"You're feeling go baby?" he prompt worried?"

"A little." She immediately plunged back to pensive, chewing the corner of her mouth.

"Do you want to tell me about the counselor?" he asked.

"There's a lot to unpack, but the biggest issue is..." Her brow wrinkled with real distress. "I don't know how to make this marriage work if you don't..." Her voice withered.

Don't love me?

Everything in him became gripped with tension. Was he incapable of love? Or merely afraid of it? Maybe if they had weathered the infertility storm without it causing such a rift between them, he might have allowed himself to be more vulnerable with her, but the more she had distanced herself, the less able he'd been to bridge that gap. He was beginning to see that now.

"If you don't know who I really am," she finished in a shaken voice.

Bound by a Surrogate Baby

Two couples. One baby. A billion-dollar scandal!

When secretary Molly agrees to be the surrogate for her best friend, heiress Sasha, she's giving her the greatest gift of all.

But what started as a simple act of kindness soon turns complicated when pregnant Molly gets promoted by her gorgeous Italian boss—to his convenient fiancée!

Don't miss Molly and Gio's story in
The Baby His Secretary Carries

When Molly goes into early labor, it's time for Sasha to become a mother to her tiny son while finally facing the still-sizzling passion between her and her estranged husband!

Enjoy Sasha and Rafael's story in
The Secret of Their Billion-Dollar Baby

Both available now!

The Secret of Their Billion-Dollar Baby

DANI COLLINS

HARLEQUIN
PRESENTS

ISBN-13: 978-1-335-59334-4

The Secret of Their Billion-Dollar Baby

Recycling programs
for this product may
not exist in your area.

Harlequin Enterprises ULC
22 Adelaide St. West, 41st Floor
Toronto, Ontario M5H 4E3, Canada
www.Harlequin.com

Printed in Lithuania

MIX
Paper | Supporting
responsible forestry
FSC® C021394

Canadian **Dani Collins** knew in high school that she wanted to write romance for a living. Twenty-five years later, after marrying her high school sweetheart, having two kids with him, working at several generic office jobs and submitting countless manuscripts, she got The Call. Her first Harlequin novel won the Reviewers' Choice Award for Best First in Series from *RT Book Reviews*. She now works in her own office, writing romance.

Books by Dani Collins

Harlequin Presents

Innocent in Her Enemy's Bed
Awakened on Her Royal Wedding Night

Bound by a Surrogate Baby

The Baby His Secretary Carries

Four Weddings and a Baby

Cinderella's Secret Baby
Wedding Night with the Wrong Billionaire
A Convenient Ring to Claim Her
A Baby to Make Her His Bride

Jet-Set Billionaires

Cinderella for the Miami Playboy

Visit the Author Profile page
at Harlequin.com for more titles.

For my wonderful editor Laurie Johnson, who surrogates my manuscript into a finished book. Thank you for all you do.

PROLOGUE

HER HAND FELT as though her bones were being crushed against themselves. The pain was acute enough to drag Alexandra Zamos toward consciousness, but she didn't want to come back through the door into reality. That's all reality was: pain.

She fluttered her eyes open and saw her stepfather. He was the one crushing her hand. Typical. One way or another, he was always trying to maintain a cruel hold on her.

A sob of repulsion rose weakly in her throat as she tried to pull away from his grip.

"She's awake! Nurse!" Her mother's voice grew distant as her heels clicked away.

That was also typical. Winnifred Humbolt always turned her back when Sasha was at her most vulnerable. She hated her for that.

She hated both of them and had gone so far as to sell herself into a new life to escape them, but had found herself imprisoned in a different type of torture.

Where was Rafael? Why wasn't he here to shield her from them?

Her heart lurched as she realized she was in a hospital. Stark fear of what she might face had her longing to sink back into oblivion, where nothing could hurt her ever again, but she heard his voice.

"Let me see her." The grit in his tone, carrying from a nearby room, made her heart swerve again.

Relief washed over her, especially because Humbolt finally released her hand. She never, ever called her stepfather by his first name, Anson. Why would she when it annoyed him so intensely to be referred to like a butler?

But now she was forced to gather up her defenses against her husband. Rafael was a formidable man. She didn't dread seeing him the way she loathed her stepfather, but she feared how easily Rafael could destroy her in other ways. He already had.

"Do you love me?"

"That was never part of our agreement."

It wasn't. For a long time, she had been able to keep her guard up around him, but over time her defenses had eroded. He'd crept under her skin like a splinter. Every tiny remark, no matter how gently delivered or kindly meant, became a stiletto to the heart.

Then she had gone and revealed how vulnerable she was to him. What a mistake! Her husband drank power like a protein shake every morning. He loved it more than he could ever love her. She should have realized that before she bared her heart to him.

She couldn't live this way anymore. She really couldn't.

"Signora Zamos?" A nurse smiled and leaned over her. "I'm going to shine this light in your eye— Sorry."

Signora? Were they still in Rome? She had assumed America, since her parents were here. How had they arrived so quickly?

Confused, Sasha tried to flinch away, but the nurse was relentless, forcing a peek into her other eye.

"What happened?" Her voice was as scuffed as a flake of skin.

"A car crash, I'm afraid. You have a concussion. Can you tell me your birthday?"

A car crash? *When?* After the gala?

"I don't remember it." She meant the crash. The last thing she remembered was taking that tiny chance at being honest, really honest, with her husband. She had thought that maybe, if he loved her, he might accept all she'd done.

Love had never been part of their agreement, though. And learning he didn't even love her like this, when she worked so hard to be the wife he wanted, destroyed her. She hadn't dared reveal the rest.

"You don't remember your birthday?" her mother was asking with alarm, looming on the other side of the bed so suddenly that Sasha recoiled.

"Please." The nurse motioned for Sasha's mother to give her space.

Winnie refused to budge, leaning closer to urge loudly, "You remember *me*, don't you? I'm your mother, Alexandra."

All Sasha could think was, *No, you're not.* Not in the ways that counted. She knew how a real mother behaved and she had been robbed on that front.

"Can you tell me your mother's name, Signora Zamos?" the nurse asked gently. "Do you know where you are?"

The nurse's English held an accent that was a mix of Italian and Tagalog, if Sasha wasn't mistaken. She presumed they were still in Rome, but the path to escape her parents for good unrolled like a red carpet in her mind. If she didn't acknowledge their place in her life, they wouldn't have one, would they?

"No." Driven by years of mistrust and manipulation, she claimed, "No. I don't know who they are."

"What about me?" The tense, masculine voice prompted the nurse to step aside, revealing Rafael.

He sat in a wheelchair. The side of his swarthy, gorgeous face was bruised. His eye was swollen and his lip cut. His arm was bandaged from elbow to wrist, his leg was in a cast, sticking straight out.

Sasha was struck dumb by horror. Hot tears pressed against the backs of her eyes. She was furious with him. She was so hurt she kind of hated him. But she also loved him, which meant that his injuries devastated her. She had nearly lost him!

But love was never part of their agreement.

He needed an heiress and an heir. He was obsessed with securing his empire. He didn't need *her*. He had her money and his successor was on its way, hopefully still safe in the belly of their surrogate.

Molly hadn't been with them, had she?

Sasha looked around with anxious confusion, panicked that she couldn't remember when or where the crash had happened.

"What day is it?" She had texted Molly yesterday that she would call her in the morning. Was this the morning after the gala?

Oh, God. If something had happened to the baby—

She couldn't take that thought. It was a last straw of anguish. She draped her forearm over her eyes, hiding from all of this, unwilling to hear what might come next.

"Alexandra," Rafael growled. "Look at me."

Someone must have pushed him closer to the bed. He took her limp hand. Her fingers felt bruised and sensitive after withstanding Humbolt's clammy crush, but Rafael's warm grip was careful if not actually tender. He guided her arm to rest their linked hands in the middle of her chest.

She couldn't help looking at him and grew worried when she realized the way he was angled to reach her hand was causing him to grimace in pain.

She withdrew her hand so he wouldn't have to extend himself.

His irises were such a dark brown they often seemed black, but they flashed with fire as he sat back and brought his hand into his lap. His mouth tightened in dismay.

His lashes were too long and thick and pretty for a man. That had always annoyed her, that he possessed such natural beauty while she had to visit salons for extensions. But she noted with distress that his jaw was stubbled with what had to be two or three days' worth of beard. His cheeks were gaunt beneath his bladelike cheekbones. His face was lined with strain, his eyes sunken from lack of sleep.

And those compelling dark eyes were trying to consume her soul.

"Do you know who I am?" he asked.

Was that a real question?

No. She gave a small shake of her head. She had never really known who he was. They were honest with each other, mostly, but never open. Never revealing.

Something tortured flashed across his expression. He reached again for her hand and rubbed his thumb restlessly into the V between her thumb and finger.

They were both battered and in pain, but there was still that tingle of energy between them. Of *life*.

"I'm your husband. Rafael." He waited a beat, watching for recognition to dawn.

Her feeble desire to protect herself from him grasped onto the charade of lost memory. It was a strong, serviceable shield that would brace her against everyone who was asking too much of her right now. She mustered a deliberately blank look.

Maybe there was wary curiosity behind it, though, because for the first time in the longest time, she felt she had stolen back a little power for herself. She had drawn a wild card, one that she could hold against her chest until it was the right time to play it.

She hadn't held a card this explosive since—

She veered from touching that raw, exposed nerve.

Take your hand from his, she told herself, but she loved his hands on her.

That had always been her downfall. From their earliest days, she had thought their physical connection would be enough to sustain her, but it wasn't. Not when her past and present were being stretched and wrapped like an elastic band around her, coiling and coiling upon itself, growing tight enough to cut off her breathing while threatening to snap altogether.

"I'm glad you're awake. I was worried." Rafael sounded sincere, but she didn't put much store into that. *Let's give the people the show they came to see*, he often said. "When can we go home?" he asked the nurse.

Sasha pulled her hand from his, earning another sharp glace from Rafael.

"She'll come home with us," her mother said. "Won't she, Daddy?"

Sasha nearly threw up.

"Yes. She's confused and needs her mother," Humbolt said firmly.

Sasha locked eyes with the nurse. "Surely there's a—"

Clinic, she was going to say, but Rafael was talking over her, staring down Humbolt.

"Alexandra is my wife. She'll come back to our home in Athens. With *me*."

"You can't look after her like that." Humbolt sent a condescending wave at Rafael's condition.

"It will be a day or two before either of them are well enough to travel," the nurse hurried to interject, trying to defuse the confrontation. "Decisions don't have to be made right this moment. The doctor will want to assess both patients and run more tests. Let's let them rest." She ushered Sasha's parents from the room.

Rafael hovered beside her, but Sasha closed her eyes and turned her face away.

He swore under his breath and she heard the orderly wheel him away.

CHAPTER ONE

Three years ago...

RAFAEL ZAMOS HAD become a chameleon capable of blending into whichever surrounding would provide him the best chance of survival.

Tonight, he'd put on his bespoke tuxedo and walked into a New York ballroom where old money elites were gathered. A young woman in a short black dress tried to check his name off a list on her tablet, but he gave her his most dispassionate, reptilian stare.

"Have a nice evening, sir," she stammered and allowed him to pass without having to say a word.

That was the funny thing about power. A lot of the time, it was something other people gave you, especially if you created the impression that you already had an abundance of it.

He didn't have as much as he wanted. He doubted he ever would. He'd been on the wrong side of power often enough in his childhood that he had an insatiable thirst for it now, to ensure he was never at anyone's mercy ever again.

That resistance and thirst had drawn him here tonight. Competitors back in Greece were beginning to see him as a threat and were flexing their muscles against him. Yet again, he was being pressured to quit rising above his station.

Rafael was beyond literal fights that left him bleeding on the ground. No, he understood that tailored suits were a type of armor and the right connections could be an impermeable shield. He hated being beholden to anyone, but strategic partnerships would reinforce the place he was carving for himself as a global player in international trade. No one closer to home was willing to align with him, but an American pillar would do nicely for now.

These snobbish circles were notoriously hard to penetrate, though. They could smell an imposter a mile off. He was already receiving the side-eye as he accepted champagne and scoped out the roomful of balding, heavyset men with bejeweled, middle-aged wives. The few youthful women were likely trophies. This wasn't an event for mistresses. It was a political fundraiser of some kind. The power behind the power.

But who the hell was *she*?

Rafael's abdomen tightened as though taking a punch while his gaze fixated on a blonde woman of midtwenties who floated to the center of the ballroom in a risqué gown of diaphanous purple. The fabric twisted from one shoulder across her breasts and around her torso before it fell in mostly see-through panels around her naked legs. Well-placed spangles on the underlay covered her nipples and mound, but it was barely decent. He could see her ass.

Which was a joy to behold. All of her was mouthwatering.

He was not the only person who noticed. Everyone turned their heads and goggled their eyes. Even the music faltered briefly, just long enough for a curse to be heard from some distant corner of the room.

A fiftyish woman in a blue gown with a skirt like a church bell bore down on the newcomer. She had to press her skirt down to lean close enough to scorch the blonde's ear.

The blonde, much to his everlasting respect, maintained a bland smile of disinterest, barely acknowledging whatever was being said as she scanned the room and landed on making eye contact with *him*.

Another blow struck his midsection, radiating heat into his chest and low into his groin.

Mine, he thought. It wasn't a conscious thought. It was far more primitive than that. It was a basic claiming that resounded in the most atavistic parts of him. Lizard brain, gut, testes.

While everyone was exchanging looks and straining to hear whatever was passing between the women, Rafael strolled over to them, eating up all those well-displayed curves and the way her aloof expression narrowed to interest in him.

"Hello, darling. I was waiting for you." He loved using phrases like that. They suggested he'd been invited and caused people like the older woman to trip into courtesy as they tried to welcome him while also trying to place him.

His accent always threw them, too. His mother had been Romanian and he had spoken Greek since childhood, then was taught English by an Australian-Indian, so there were subtle undertones that always had people blinking in confusion.

"You look beautiful. Shall we dance?" he asked his new obsession.

The blonde used her thick lashes to screen, then reveal aquamarine eyes that were likely contacts, but he found her whole package of unapologetic sexuality irresistible.

"The dancing starts after dinner, sir," the older woman said in a corrective tone.

Rafael immediately despised her for it. He would not be thwarted.

Fortunately, the blonde seemed to feel the same. She offered him fingers that were taloned with long, dark purple nails. "I thought you'd never ask."

If Rafael had been a man who believed in such things, he would have called this love at first sight. In reality, it was animal attraction and like finding like, but it was heady. This woman not only knew how to command attention, she wielded her influence with fascinating ruthlessness.

He steered her through the formally set tables and the murmuring crowd until they reached the dance floor. It was occupied by a raised dais and a podium that would presumably be removed after the speeches. Behind it, the orchestra was working through a mix-and-mingle set with a subdued, lazy tempo that didn't require proper steps.

Rafael slid his hand from the woman's hip to her lower back, liking that she wore such tall heels because it put her nearly at eye level with him. She pressed closer and twined her arms around his neck, allowing him to fold his arms all the way around her narrow waist, securing her pelvis to his. She offered an amused smile at the stir they provoked.

"Your gown is making an impression."

"On you?" She arched a hairbreadth closer, well aware she was causing a specific stir in him.

"On everyone," he clarified. But yes. Absolutely on him.

She was pure nitroglycerin. He would have to be very careful, but he wanted to bottle her and keep her forever.

"It's not just the gown. It's who's wearing it." Her fingertips traced a line along the back of his collar. Her tickling touch caused his scalp to tighten along with every muscle in his body.

"Are you not supposed to be here?" he asked idly. "Welcome to the club, angel."

"Did you crash this party?" she asked, pretending to be scandalized. "I think I just fell in love." She knew how to use her lashes to best effect, sweeping them down so her gaze traversed his shoulders and chest in a way that felt like a caress. A claiming.

He firmed his hold on her, enjoying the small hitch in her breath and the way her gaze flashed back to his, filled with startled heat.

She didn't know what to do with the fact that he was having the same effect on her that she was having on him. He liked that. He liked it very much.

"You don't know who I am?" She seemed skeptical of that.

"A goddess, I presume."

"A demon, more like. But I was not only invited, I was given strict orders to wear something appropriate, since I'm expected to stand with my mother behind my stepfather as he accepts his participation ribbon for being a good political donor." The corners of her mouth curled with bitter satisfaction at how mercilessly she'd clapped back.

Her rebellious spirit was both a draw and a warning, one he didn't let deter him.

"And who is the man looking like he wishes he was holding dueling pistols instead of champagne glasses?" Rafael had been a target from his earliest years. He clocked any threat, even lightweights like that privileged crash test dummy glaring daggers at them. The man was roughly Rafael's age, approaching thirty, well-dressed. Rafael was certain the man was richer and better connected, but Rafael could take him if it came to it.

"Do we call him a man if he agrees to marry the woman his father picks out for him?" She tilted her head in mock curiosity. "His mother still buys his underwear."

"You're his fiancée?" That was news he didn't care for. His hands unconsciously tightened on her.

"Not yet." Her fingertips moved to the hollow at the base of her skull. She caressed and explored. Pressed with invitation. "You should kiss me now, while I'm still unattached."

She was toying with him for her own purpose—he knew that, but he was willing to take the kiss she offered purely for the thrill of it.

It was more than thrilling. As he met her parted lips with his own, electric heat shot through him. He would typically be a gentleman and allow her to set the pace, but with her, he tilted his head to capture her soft lips more thoroughly. He stopped dancing and cupped her head and *took*. He learned the shape of her pouted lips and the texture of her tongue and the erotic taste of her mouth.

He did everything he could to imprint himself on her.

Take me. Have all of me. Everything.

That willingness to give up all of himself rang bells of alarm within him, but the receptive tag of her tongue sent pure lightning into his groin, emptying his brain. He reacted in a borderline barbarian way, excited by how eager she was.

Yes, she was a potent and dangerous woman. She could

strip him of all his hard gains, but in this moment of carnal greed, he didn't care. Her nails curled into his jacket as she dragged him closer, demanding more of him. He was beyond willing to let her drain him dry.

Hell, he was ready to have sex with her right here in the middle of the dance floor with her parents and the rest of the world watching.

Was that all this was for her, though? A show?

He dragged his head up, mouth burning, gaze on the lipstick smudged across her mouth.

"You're using me." It wasn't an accusation. It was a statement of fact, but he kept her hips pinned to his, both to hide and soothe his raging erection.

"Not entirely," she breathed against his chin. Her curves pressed willingly against him. She blinked in a way that suggested she was as blown away by their kiss as he was. "I wanted to know how that would feel. Making a scene while we did it was icing on the cake."

He wasn't sure he believed her, but his focus had narrowed to a very basic, libidinous desire to mate with her. Right now.

"Come with me." It was a command, but it was also a question. A test. Was she really as carried away as he was? Would she quit showboating for these pearl-clutchers and take this to its next steps?

"I thought you'd never ask." She slid her hand down his sleeve to clasp his hand, then led him from the ballroom, ignoring the gasps they left in their wake.

He was likely nuking any chance he had at finding a business partner among them, but he didn't care, not when she had become his entire reason for existing.

Thankfully, he was staying in the hotel's penthouse. It

was an extravagant move, given how overleveraged he was, but it had been another means of reducing friction when he entered the ballroom. He tapped his card to the elevator mechanism and they shot upward.

"Who are you?" he asked her.

"Do you really want to talk?" She slid into his arms.

He did not. He had never had a blind hookup in his life, always careful he wasn't leaving a flank unprotected, but as he succumbed to the urge to kiss her, he understood how Troy had fallen. Power and lust were two sides of the same coin. Spend one, lose the other.

He fought allowing lust to win, but she was taut against him again, and this barely there dress of hers was almost like stroking her naked skin. Everything in him wanted to claim her. If he'd had a condom on him, he would have had her in the elevator.

The doors slid open with a ping and he dragged her down the hall and into his suite, prepared to shout, "Get out!" if he saw a single maid, but it was empty.

He pressed her to the wall and discovered exactly how well matched they were as they both gave in to this devastating passion. His body ignited, prompting him to yank at the buttons of his new jacket, possibly tearing them as he fought to free himself.

She pushed the jacket off his shoulders, then began searching for the buttons between the pleats of his shirt.

Her skin was much easier to access. He dragged up the cobweb of her skirt. There were yards and yards of the stuff, but it was deliciously cool and soft. Almost as delicious as the smooth thigh he eventually found.

She broke away from their kiss to gasp for breath.

"No?" He would *die*.

"No. I mean, yes. Touch me," she said in a voice that shuddered with want.

He couldn't help the rumble of an animalistic growl that resounded in his chest. She was so soft, so smooth, warm and undeniably feminine. He found the thin line of a flesh-toned thong at her hip and watched his hand as he followed it.

The sheer purple of her skirt bunched against his wrist as he arrived at the crease next to her mound, so warm and smooth. So sensitive and responsive her breath shook as he drew light patterns there. She bit her bottom lip, eyes heavy lidded.

"You want this?" His voice was lost in the well of his chest.

"I want everything," she whispered. "Except talking."

He snorted. "Tell me if you need me to stop, then. Otherwise, I'm taking us all the way."

He barely gave her the chance to exhale a potent, "Yes," before he swooped to capture her mouth again. At the same time, he broke the band on the miniscule triangle of silk and claimed what he found behind it.

She jolted and moaned into his mouth, whimpering as he pressed his palm over her mound, waiting for her to press back before he began to explore. The abundant moisture he discovered nearly blinded him with excitement. The way she trembled and moaned nearly undid him.

He was so aroused, he could have taken her to the floor and lost himself in her right here, but he was determined to keep hold of some trace of control. If she wanted all the lust in him, she could have it. She would not steal his power over himself, though. No, he would have the upper hand here, not her.

To that end, he deepened his caress, sliding his fingertip around and across the swollen knot that made delicious sounds pang in her throat. Around and around and around until she was arched and bunching his shirt in her fists and moaning with abandon into his mouth.

Oh, that was lovely. He pressed his wide palm over the soaked heat of her again, holding it steady for the rock of her hips as she rode out a shuddering climax. Her pulses and throbs were so intense, he felt them like a hammer strike in the tip of his erection, but he didn't allow himself to fall over the edge. Not yet.

"You're using me," this stranger had accused her and, yes, Alexandra had been using him to scandalize her mother.

But once he had kissed her? Now?

She was using him all right, but it was purely for a type of pleasure she hadn't known was possible for her. She had gone into that ballroom feeling so trapped, she might as well have been a genie compressed into a bottle. She'd barely been able to breathe, but now she was panting and flying. Soaring.

She was free in a way she hadn't expected to ever feel. Not with all the hang-ups she had around sex. Her beauty and sexuality were weapons she had learned to use to disconcert and humiliate, so they couldn't be turned on her. They had never been sources of *pleasure*.

Until now.

Until this stranger showed her what her body was capable of.

With charged kisses and languid caresses, he was teaching her to not only embrace her sensuality, but express it with abandon. She stroked her hands over his bared chest and delicately sucked his tongue.

In some ways, it was terrifying to let him take these liberties and pull forth such a wild response, but it was a step forward that she grasped with both hands. This was only for the one night anyway. It's not like he would toy with her this way forever.

He took her at her word about not talking. As her body wilted in the aftermath of a life-altering orgasm, he scooped her up and carried her to the bedroom. He stood her beside the bed, then stepped into the bathroom to retrieve a box of condoms that he threw onto the mattress.

In a kind of haze, she turned to offer her zip, lifting her hair out of the way.

He obliged by lowering it, slowly, setting kisses along her spine and leaving a hot pool of breath against her skin, all the way to her lower back.

Shivering, she dropped the gown and stepped out of her shoes. Her thong was already gone. She slipped onto the bed and turned to face him.

He was stripping without taking his eyes off her, skimming away trousers and boxers in one move, revealing he was very aroused. His erection was steely and dark, his expression barely civilized.

As he set a hand and a knee on the mattress, starting to loom over her, she retreated slightly, daunted. Her hand instinctually pressed at his chest.

He froze. "Changing your mind?"

"I'm not sure." She wanted this. She did. But she had forgotten how physical sex was. How overwhelming. How vulnerable it made her feel.

"That's fine." His expression grew shuttered. "I'm disappointed, but not angry." He shifted to the side so she could rise off the bed if she wanted to.

Ironically, the fact that he was so willing to stop this late in the game made her trust him more than she had a split second ago.

What was she supposed to do? Go the rest of her life without ever having sex again? It had already been eight years. Here was a man who was not only respectful enough to stop but who turned her on like no one else ever had.

"Will you—" she cleared her throat "—let me be on top?"

He dropped onto his back and folded his arms behind his head. "Help yourself."

"I might stop again if I get nervous," she warned, eyeing the banquet of tanned skin stretched firmly across the sort of muscles that belonged on an athlete. A swimmer, maybe. He had wide shoulders and well-defined abs. A light pattern of hair lay flat against his skin, thicker against his breastbone and thinning as it extended to his navel.

His thighs were equally tanned and well-built, but she only noticed that in the periphery. She was studying his erection, hesitantly reaching out to draw a shy line down the length with her fingertip, both amused and intimidated by the way the thick muscle twitched under her touch.

"Are you a virgin?" he asked with puzzlement.

"No." She choked on a harsh laugh. If he only knew her history, he'd swallow his tongue before suggesting that. "No, it's just been a long time for me."

She slid closer and he gathered her atop him. He was a hot beach that felt like pure decadence to lie upon. Shifting against him produced sensations that were as erotic as the caress of a tropical surf. The satin-covered muscles beneath her called to the most primitive woman in her, teasing her to braid her legs with his so the damp tip of his erection sat in the crease of her mound. Her loins throbbed with awareness as she lowered her head to kiss him.

She knew she wouldn't hesitate again. This was too good. She rocked her mouth against his in deep, unhurried kisses.

She might have made a mistake, however, in allowing him to have both hands free. He took full advantage, skimming his fingertips over her back and buttocks, sensitizing her to his touch before he erased all those tickles with a firmer stroke that ironed her onto his front.

Then he became even more deliberate, palming her backside in a way designed to reignite her passion. When one hand cruised up her waist and sought her breast, she angled so he could cup the swell and toy with her nipple.

She moaned, subtly writhing with a need for *more*. More friction. More of those wicked caresses of his thumb against her nipple. More intimacy and intention and sinful attention where she longed to feel it most.

She brought her knees up so she straddled his thighs, rising to reach for the box of condoms. She offered one to him.

"Sure?"

She nodded.

He held her gaze as he took it, bit the corner, and ripped it open. As he rolled it on, old ghosts swirled through her psyche, but he moved his hand to the seam of her sex and all other thoughts disappeared. Her eyes fluttered closed and the only thing she was aware of was the way his thumb lightly traced a tantalizing line of sensations that made her feel like a flower blossoming open.

As need coiled through her, her hips rocked, seeking a deeper touch and the fulfillment she knew he could offer.

"Take me when you're ready." His smoky command was so husky and mesmerizing, she couldn't do anything but obey.

He held himself for her and she guided herself onto his length, letting out a soft cry of ecstasy as she sank down, stretched and caressed and connected to him in a way that left her wordless. Dazzled.

She braced her hands on his chest and stared into his eyes. They'd been all pupils a moment ago and were now glittering slits behind the tangle of his thick lashes. He was inordinately handsome, with clean-shaven cheeks beneath high cheekbones, a hawkish nose, and a mouth that could spawn a thousand fantasies. His brows were heavy, his jaw strong, his rakish hair rumpled by her fingers.

She could look at this face for the rest of her life, she thought whimsically.

His hands were drawing absent patterns on her thighs, but climbed to her hips, skimmed along her waist, then cupped her breasts. He circled her nipples with the pads of his thumbs.

Her body reacted by shivering and tightening around him. She leaned into his touch, then bent the rest of the way down to seal her mouth to his.

That seemed to be his undoing. He rolled her beneath him and began to thrust, pausing when she gasped in awe at the joyous pleasure that crashed through her.

"Don't stop!" she cried with anguish.

That was it. His body gathered and he became her whole world, seeming determined to create a memory she would never forget. Determined to claim her in every way—with his mouth, with his touch, with his sex. With the sound of his voice and the smell of his skin.

She couldn't track all the sensations or all the ways she was losing herself to him in those heated moments. She only knew later that that's what had happened to her. He destroyed her in the most sensual way possible. She welcomed it. By the end, when he dared to slow his strokes, holding her on the precipice of culmination, she was utterly at his mercy.

"Please," she whispered.

His fingers tangled in her hair. He held her for a long, drugging kiss, holding them both in this magical place of pure sensation. She felt like a single, exposed nerve, the very air almost too much on her hot, damp skin.

He withdrew and returned with a powerful flex of his hips, propelling her into such a powerful orgasm, she screamed.

His hips crashed into hers again and again, increasing the power of her release. He was off the leash and it was glorious.

Ecstasy was her new home. It gripped her and imbued her and emanated from her as he lost his rhythm and melded their flesh. He shouted with triumph and the pulses within her echoed the slam of her heart.

CHAPTER TWO

AFTER HIS ORGASM turned him inside out, and Rafael was exhausted on the bed beside her, he had a disturbing moment of feeling vanquished. *Beaten.*

But when he turned his head on the pillow, she was looking at the ceiling with an expression that reflected what he was feeling. Awe?

She slid him a look from the corner of her eye and immediately rearranged her features into smug amusement.

"Well, that was something, wasn't it?" She pulled the edge of the bedspread across her middle and curled toward him. "Thank you."

"It was very much my pleasure." He discarded the condom into the wastebasket and fell back onto the bed beside her, too sated to move more than that.

"I should leave." She sat up and her hair fell forward to hide most of her profile.

He studied her curved spine and couldn't resist setting his thumb and middle fingertip against the dimples at the top of her backside.

"You don't have to," he heard himself say. "Unless you need to get back to your party?"

"Can you imagine?" She kept the bedspread secured to her breasts, but braced a hand behind herself so she twisted to face him. "What do I look like right now? A ghoul from the crypt? A drunken clown?"

He likely wore more of her lipstick than she did. Her eyes were smudged and smoky and heavy lidded.

"You're sexy as hell." It was only the truth, but saying it caused a strange tremor in his chest. "I'm sure you know that."

"It's still nice to hear it. When it's sincere." Her pensive gaze lifted to the closed drapes.

He was equally disturbed. This had been the best sex of his life, which made it a purgatory of sorts. It was a memory that could imprison him for eternity.

He dismissed that melodramatic thought, attributing the heightened eroticism to their being strangers, and reminded himself she had only slept with him to irritate her parents.

Which didn't bother him, but didn't *not* bother him.

"I'll stay long enough for a shower, if you don't mind." Whatever blue mood had started to take hold in her was discarded with a careless smile. She threw off the bedspread and rose to walk into the bathroom.

He heard the toilet and the tap and imagined she was using the complementary makeup remover pads. When the shower started, he quit pretending he wasn't going to join her.

"Oh, hello," she said when he opened the glass door and joined her inside the marble-tiled enclosure. It was more than big enough for both of them with nozzles and sprays from all directions.

"Hello to you. Blue eyes." He cupped her face, looking into irises that were now the color of a clear sky over a mountain lake.

She reacted to his touch with a grasp of his wrists and a

dazzling sparkle inside those pretty eyes. Her lips parted in invitation.

"I'm Rafael," he told her.

"Alexandra." The minx guided one of his hands down to shake hers. "It's a pleasure to meet you."

"Isn't it?"

It really was. For the next seventy-two hours, they barely left each other's sight. They shared the bed and the robes, the shower and meals and bottles of wine.

The concierge delivered more condoms and a handful of other necessities, but housekeeping was turned away and all calls ignored. Occasionally, Alexandra shrugged on one of his shirts, but more often than not, they were naked on the wrecked bed, dozing, talking about innocuous topics—movies and travel and whether horoscopes had any basis in reality, but mostly, they made love.

He learned that her feet were ticklish and she was not only the stepdaughter of a Very Rich Man, she was rich in her own right. Her father's family had amassed a fortune in publishing over several generations. Her mother's family were also Old Money with ties to industrial age railway tycoons.

"My father died when I was young. I don't remember him," she said with a philosophical shrug. "Humbolt pounced on Mother like a hyena on a wounded wildebeest and took control of her, her fortune, *and* my trust. That money he was being lauded for donating? *Mine*. What a paragon." Her lip curled in contempt.

"But he doesn't control you."

"Not for lack of trying, believe me." She quit tracing the pattern in the headboard and rolled onto her stomach so the sheet twisted around her. "What about you? What will I learn when I stalk you online after this?"

"I was born in Romania. My mother brought me to Greece to find my father who was Greek. We never found him. She passed away when I was five. I went into foster care, bounced through some group homes, then landed with a Greek couple who chose to adopt me. I grew up on the outskirts of Athens."

"Were they nice? Your adoptive parents?" She was giving him doe eyes, which made him uncomfortable.

"Yes." They'd tried to be, not that he'd known what to do with it. He'd had many a hard knock by then. His mother had barely scraped by, then died overnight. He'd been teased at school and scrapped his way through it. His adoptive parents had been withdrawn for their own reasons so Rafael had never fully seen himself as their son.

"My father died when I was seventeen. Heart attack." Rafael couldn't help the bitterness that invaded his voice and quickly averted his thoughts from that day. "I took over the family business, but there were vultures who wanted it for themselves. They tried to use the fact I was adopted against me, saying I wasn't legitimately my father's son, that I wasn't Greek, or not Greek enough. So I keep that information in my bio online, next to my brief arrest for breaking and entering."

"Oh." Her brows went up. "You are colorful."

"It was a misunderstanding. Or, I should say, another attempt to keep me from taking over the business. It was soon cleared up."

"What kind of business?" She cocked her head.

"At that time, a marine service operation for small and midrange vessels. There was always potential for more, but my father was never able to maximize it. There was a cartel who kept him in his place. When he died, they thought they wanted the company more than I did. They were wrong."

Her eyes widened. "What did you do?"

Whatever he had to. He deliberately sidestepped that question, trotting out the patter he gave any reporter who asked a similar question.

"Thankfully, like any adolescent, I was into gaming. When I wasn't working at the shop under my father, or going to school, I made videos. I'd become an influencer of sorts. I was making decent money, enough to help with my parents' mortgage. My father didn't know that. My mother handled all the books at the business and at home. She also knew that if these enforcers realized we were getting ahead, they'd put more pressure on us so she kept it under her hat. My father didn't live to see it, but having the house paid for gave me something to leverage when I took over the business. I was able to hire security and modernize. That set us up for growth."

He didn't mention the particularly ugly knife fight that had served as a warning that he was not the pushover his father had been.

"Recently, we expanded into larger ships and shipping beyond the Med. Zamos International? Heard of it?"

She wrinkled her nose in apology. "I have now."

"I'm still seen as an upstart," he admitted. "I've ceased to be a minnow that can easily be swallowed, but that makes me a genuine rival to the bigger players. I crashed your stepfather's party looking for American connections into the Eastern Seaboard, to shore up my position."

"Oh, dear. I have to be honest, Rafael. Stealing me away like this?" She drew a circle to indicate their love palace. "It has screwed your chances with everyone in that room. Pun intended. Humbolt can't disown me for misbehaving, but he can punish my friends by blacklisting them."

"I knew what I was risking when I approached you." Did he, though? He wasn't angry at her, per se, but he was angry he had allowed his libido to rule him. The longer he stayed here with her, the more opportunities he was allowing to slip away.

"Let me make it up to you," she purred and sprawled across him while she began kissing her way south.

Carnal hunger dug its claws into him, dimming his ability to think.

Last time, he promised himself, and crooked his legs open so she could kneel between his thighs.

"For you," Rafael said while she was dozing off their morning lovemaking.

Sasha thought he had risen to let in their breakfast, but he set a gorgeous bouquet of orchids and bird-of-paradise onto the night table.

She sat up, stomach lurching sickly, but hid her humiliation behind a bland smile. "I've overstayed my welcome. You should have said."

"Not at all. They're not from me." When his flinty gaze met hers, her heart stalled. Was he jealous? Suspicious?

He plucked the card with two fingers and offered it to her.

Her nerveless fingers didn't want to work. She wound up tearing the tiny envelope to withdraw the card that read, *Call your mother.*

"Mother." She flicked the card off the bed. "Took her

long enough to find me. You weren't on the guest list, though. Were you?" She dragged the sheet across her breasts and bunched the pillows behind her so she could slouch into them with a sigh and a wry smile. "That must have annoyed her, having to ask around to find out who you were. Now everyone knows you were an interloper. She'll use that against you. Sorry." She wrinkled her nose at him.

He made a noise of acknowledgment that also rang with discontent. "Coffee?"

"There you go seducing me again." She was trying to return to their easy banter, but seriously, everything about him seduced her. The belt of his robe was negligently tied at his waist, leaving the lapels gaping to reveal his tanned chest.

He countered with, "I can't seem to help myself," but his tone wasn't as light as it had been. Reality was permeating the air like the perfume of the orchids.

She watched him amble from the room and even his silhouette of wide shoulders and the laconic slap of his bare feet made her ache with longing. She knew she ought to leave, but couldn't seem to make herself.

"It's hot," he said when he returned and set the two cups of coffee beside the bouquet.

Sasha wanted to knock the flowers to the floor, but they were only a symbol of the thing she really didn't want—to speak to her mother. She didn't want to leave this bubble of intimacy and pleasure. To leave *him*.

He didn't walk around and climb into the bed beside her, the way he'd done most other times he returned to this bed. He sat on the edge of the mattress facing her.

"Exactly how will your mother try to make me uncomfortable?" he asked.

Oh. They were facing reality, were they? How disappointing.

"Socially," she replied. "She'll have you cut from invite lists to galas and events."

"I'll go anyway." He dismissed her reply with a shrug.

A sunny ball of hope broke open in her chest, then a shadow moved across it.

"Humbolt is the greater threat. He's spent twenty years using my father's money to curry business connections and political favors. He has a lot of sway when he wants to use it. God, I hate him." She shoved her legs out straight as though she could kick that man out of her life once and for all. And now he was trying to marry her off to that insipid—

She sucked in a breath of realization and sat up, curling her legs beneath her so she knelt as she faced Rafael. She set her hand on the white velvet of the robe that coated his strong shoulder.

His cheek ticked in awareness that she had let the sheet drop and was naked before him, but his gaze remained locked with hers.

"Yes?"

"You and I should marry." She was shocked that such words spilled from her lips, but they felt right.

"Oh?" He used the excuse of leaning to pick up his mug to force her hand to fall away. "I was planning to wait until after I turned thirty-five."

"How old are you now?"

"Twenty-nine. But I have hundreds of goals ahead of

me before I settle down. Thousands. *Billions* to acquire," he added with dry significance.

"I don't want to marry, either." She dragged the sheet in front of her, but stayed kneeling on the bed, gaze turned inward while she spoke her thoughts aloud. "When Humbolt realized I was coming up to twenty-four, he also realized that puts me a year away from taking control of my trust. I could have taken the reins sooner by marrying anytime, but I couldn't stand the idea of a husband. I still don't want one, but Humbolt has handpicked this son of his crony. He thinks this dolt will keep me in line and allow him continued access to my fortune. Mother wants everything done properly, of course. A year-long engagement and all that nonsense."

"This isn't the Dark Ages. Tell them no and wait it out," Rafael suggested as though it was just that easy.

"I was planning to, but Humbolt holds the purse strings and uses them to bring me to heel. I've put aside a nest egg," she confided, proud of the way she'd embezzled from her own funds. "It's a hoard of jewelry in a safe-deposit box. I'm like a *dragon*," she said on a chuckle, then sobered. "It's enough to keep me going for a while, but it's insurance for something else." She veered from letting herself worry about publicity and legal fees. It wouldn't happen. She was always really careful to keep her secret very much a secret. "Mostly I *hate* the idea of walking away and allowing him to keep my money. So I have to fight for it. But the last time I outright defied him, he had me placed on a psych hold so—"

Rafael swore. "Are you serious?"

"Yes. I was still a teenager. I was supposed to go back to boarding school in Switzerland, but instead I went to

Ibiza for six months." That was the cover story she always told when referring to that time of her life. "I don't think he would go to such an extreme length now, given he's trying to marry me off, but he'll find some other way to make my life miserable. I refuse to let him *win*, though. It's *my* money. And he's been using it—and me—for his own gain for almost twenty years. I don't *want* to put up with another year of him and Mother holding me at gunpoint."

"How much money?" he asked curiously.

"A hundred and fifty million. I get the balance when I have a baby or turn thirty. Five hundred million, give or take. I imagine that sort of asset would be helpful to you, if you had access to it?" She fluttered her lashes at him, knowing it damned well would.

He was impervious to her flirting, though. Her lover was gone. Rafael might as well be wearing a three-piece suit and a fresh shave. He was all business.

"It would," he acknowledged with an unreadable expression.

"My sense is that you'd like to continue having sex with me? At least for a while? Am I wrong about that?"

"I was going to suggest we continue this affair." His cheek ticked again.

"Then here's what I propose. I'll tell Mother this was a final fling and I'm ready to play ball. That will distract them long enough for you and I to negotiate our prenup."

His brows went up, but she wasn't an idiot. She'd had to look after herself once before and knew how to do it.

"We'll marry in secret then, *bam*!" She punched into her

own palm. "We'll hit them with it in a few weeks." She was already laughing at the shock on their faces.

"That seems like a lot of unnecessary drama and sub-terfuge."

"Would you rather announce our engagement and watch Humbolt use my money to try to destroy you?"

"Is that a threat?"

"*No*. I'm telling you what kind of man I'm dealing with. But if you don't want to marry me, that's fine." His rebuff stung, though. It really did. "I'll find another way," she decided. "Another man. I had made up my mind not to marry so I didn't even consider this avenue, but now that I have, I'll shop for my own docile but useful idiot..." She threw off the sheet and scooted to the edge of the mattress.

Rafael stuck out his arm to stop her, then leaned across to set his coffee back on the night table. "I didn't say I don't want to. Tell me why you're so averse to marriage."

"Because I don't want to be controlled by anyone." She looked pointedly at the arm barring her exit from the bed. "Least of all a husband."

"I'm capable of reason. And I'll need an heir eventually. It sounds as though you will, too."

Her heart contracted along with her pupils, turning the room blurry at the edges. Pure adrenaline stung her veins, the kind that urged flight. She fought revealing the panic that quickened her breath and jerked her gaze free of his. She plucked at the sleeve of his robe, silently requesting he remove his arm.

He drew back and she rose to pick up the shirt he had discarded across the back of a chair. She shrugged herself into it, frantically thinking while she buttoned it.

"Having a baby purely to take control of my fortune is

wrong. Let's see how we get on," she suggested, noticing the tremble in her hands as she rolled the cuffs up to expose her wrists. "If we're still married in a few years, we'll discuss children. There's every chance we won't be. I'm a rebellious spirit. Some would call me a hellion."

"I noticed," he assured her with a brief glint of amusement. "But I appreciate your candor. In fact—" he narrowed his eyes "—this would only work if we are completely honest with each other. You can't play any of these bait and switch games with me. We need to be able to trust each other. You understand that, don't you?" His tone was still light, but she heard the warning in it.

A shiver of premonition chased down her spine.

She trusted him. Physically. She would do some digging to be sure she could trust him with her money. With her heart, though? With her *secrets*? She doubted she would ever fully trust a man again.

"There's a difference between being honest and being transparent," she said. "I can promise to be honest with you. Faithful, definitely." She had a bleak sense that she would never feel this same desire for any other man, so that was an easy promise to make. "But I will choose how much of myself and my past I want to share with you. By the same token, it will be your choice how much of yourself you share with me."

"You're starting to sound too good to be true, Alexandra." He was still sitting on the bed and leaned back on his hands, robe gaping to expose his inner thighs. He was barely decent and so sexy, her mouth dried.

"'Good' is the last word people would use to describe me," she assured him.

"I happen to know you're *very* good. Come here and show me how good. Seal the deal," he coaxed.

"I *just* got dressed."

In his shirt and nothing else.

Get used to it, she thought. She was about to use him and his trappings as a shield, but she would have little protection against *him*.

Nevertheless, even though her heart was pounding in apprehension, her feet took her to the bed.

"You really want to do this? Marry?" She set her hands on his shoulders and her knees on the mattress, straddling his lap.

"I do." His wide palms immediately climbed beneath the crisp cotton of the shirt, claiming her naked skin.

It's worth it, she told herself. *Whatever happens, it will be worth it for this.*

Two weeks later, Rafael walked with his new bride into a Manhattan mansion.

Had he had reservations about marrying her? Probably not as many as he ought to. When they had parted after their three-day sex fest, he had promised to call her, but had thought about getting on a plane straight back to Greece. He had a lot to protect and could have made any excuse to go home and guard it.

The minute she was out of his sight, however, he wanted her back. That was the uncomfortable truth that he kept to himself as he lingered in New York.

They'd seen each other intermittently as they met with lawyers and stole a few passionate interludes. Each time, he had grown more fascinated with her. More eager to have her with him all day, every day. Every *night*.

There were crude expressions for this level of desire-related impulsiveness. A distant part of himself understood he was operating on pheromones and ego. She was rich and beautiful and alluring. Any man would want her, but she was clearly capable of acting in a calculated fashion to get what she wanted.

That side of her was equally fascinating to him, though. She knew how to direct her lawyers so they were very thorough in how well they protected her, ensuring she had several avenues out of this marriage that wouldn't break her financially. This wasn't her first rodeo, as the Americans said, which prompted him to say, "You seem to know what you're doing in a boardroom. Why have you never put your lawyers onto your stepfather?"

"So he could spend my money fighting me? And use it to run a smear campaign against me?" She combed square nails, which were now a bubblegum pink, through her loose blond hair.

Rafael wasn't oblivious to the sort of things men said about women, especially when they were trying to crush them in court, but she seemed to embrace the reputation of a scarlet woman, so what else could intimidate her badly enough that she would rather avoid it?

"Putting you on him will be much more effective," she said, smoothing his lapel. "I've done my homework, you know. Once Humbolt realizes who he's dealing with, he'll start to mind his manners. Did you really steal a boat from a mafia don?"

"That is a colorful way for the press to spin my exercising a contract clause. I took possession of a ship when the repairs went unpaid." Had he also set the man up for arrest, thereby making it impossible for him to make his payments? Perhaps. But that was between him and his very unbothered conscience.

"Hmm, well, I can't wait to see how Humbolt reacts when he realizes this particular ship has been commandeered by a pirate." Her mauve-colored lips tilted into a smirk.

Oddly, the fact she made no bones about using him against her stepfather reassured him. He knew exactly where they both stood.

He had also done his homework and was pleased to learn that, along with the financial advantage of leveraging against her trust fund, he was marrying a woman who had connections to aristocracy, heiresses, and socialites around the globe. Alexandra might be named in more than one celebrity clickbait story, or wear scanty outfits to upper-crust galas, but her scandals were deliberate. She knew exactly what was expected in every setting and would help him blend seamlessly into those places himself.

He was quite satisfied with this arrangement of theirs, even when she said at the courthouse before they spoke their vows, "I will promise to honor you, but I can't promise to obey. Also, I'm growing fond of you, but I will probably never love you."

Perhaps he should have asked her why not, but that would risk her telling him that she could see through his tailored morning suit to the gutter rat he'd once been.

"Good," he said instead, meaning it. Love was a liability. People you loved could be used against you. Love made you helpless. "I need someone who is self-sufficient and won't ask me for things I'm incapable of offering. You are the yin to my yang, Alexandra."

Their vows had seemed moot at that point. They understood each other perfectly, right down to their mutual enjoyment of the commotion they created as they arrived in the sitting room of the mansion, where well-dressed couples were gathered for what was supposed to be Alexandra's engagement brunch.

Along with Alexandra's parents, her pseudo fiancé was there along with a handful of other middle-aged and older couples.

Alexandra's hand tightened in his, sending a frisson of warning through Rafael. He followed her startled glance to a man in his late forties, but she was already looking elsewhere, smiling with vicious joy at the way everyone had frozen in shock.

Their audience was taking in their joined hands and the swallowtail jacket that Rafael wore with an ivory vest and striped trousers. Alexandra wore a demure, figure-hugging dress in oyster white that ended below her knees. A short cape topped it, falling from her shoulders to her elbows.

She was classy and willowy and unabashedly smug as she stated, "There's been a misunderstanding. When I said I was ready to marry, I meant that I had found the husband I want." She smoothed her free hand along the sleeve of his jacket.

"No," Winnie Humbolt said in a gust of appalled disbelief. "I won't allow it."

"It's done." Rafael looked with suitable adoration at his entrancing bride. He could see she was having the time of her life dropping this bomb, and he couldn't help the rush of pride that he could give her this. "We've come from the courthouse."

Her mother raked in a gasp and looked as though she wanted to faint like a Victorian dowager onto the nearest couch. Humbolt was turning crimson, flapping his lips, nearly apoplectic.

"We'll have it annulled," Humbolt stammered. He shook with rage as he waggled his finger. "You're not in your right mind. You have a history."

"Try it." Rafael snapped his head around to skewer the man with his most lethal glower. "Try to take my wife from me. Try to harm her. See what happens." He had never been so sincere in his readiness to kill a man.

Humbolt's color drained. "Don't come into my home and threaten me."

"But it's not yours, is it?" Alexandra said in mock apology for having to correct him. "My name is on every piece of real estate that you live in. Now that I'm married, I've sent the paperwork to the various institutions, letting them know that I will control my assets from now on."

"You can't—" Humbolt started to bluster, but Rafael overrode him.

"I've put my own team onto performing a full audit," Rafael warned. "Don't bother trying to squirrel anything away. If Alexandra wishes to let you continue living here, that is her choice, but do be careful how you treat her going forward. I protect what's mine." He switched to a much sweeter tone when he asked her, "Do you need to pack anything for our honeymoon, darling?"

"I don't need anything but you from now on." She was gushing for their audience's sake, but he lapped it up all the same. "We'll be in the Maldives, but we won't be taking calls. Newlyweds." She sent a squinched smile at the group of slack-jawed faces.

"Alexandra!" her mother cried as they started to turn away. "Are you pregnant? Is that why you've married him?"

Alexandra jolted as though a spear had landed in her back.

"No," she choked out as she turned. "I married him to get away from you, Mother. I thought that was obvious. Also, because he's good in bed." She put on a moue of affection as she gazed up at Rafael. "That's more than she can say about *her* husband."

"I'll fight this," Humbolt warned. "You'll be sorry."

"I'm sure you can make all of us very sorry if you start muckraking." Alexandra shot that at him with a blast of ice from her eyes. "I suggest you cool off and think about whether it's worth it before you do anything rash."

Did she flash a look toward that fortyish man? Or was that Rafael's imagination?

He would never know. Alexandra tugged on his hand, saying facetiously over her shoulder, "Thank you for your warm and sincere congratulations. Goodbye!"

CHAPTER THREE

THEIR HONEYMOON LASTED a year, until the following May.

Oh, they had their spats. Rafael had not risen from being picked up off the street and stuck in an orphanage, to middle class, to obscenely wealthy without possessing self-serving, driven, and occasionally ruthless attributes. He didn't apologize for that, but he learned to restrain his worst impulses for the sake of a peaceful marriage.

Alexandra *was* difficult at times, but it came from being a passionate person who had been materially spoiled all her life. She had a strong grasp of her own worth and wasn't afraid to hold her ground when she decided she wanted something.

For the most part, however, they were aligned in their goal, which was to become a force to be reckoned with. While he accumulated the power of money, she nurtured their connections and influence.

Rafael knew why he needed the security of being dominant and untouchable. He never again wanted to be as vulnerable as he had been in his early years. Alexandra hadn't ever been cold and hungry, sleeping behind dumpsters, though. She hadn't been knocked around for being unable to read and write, then for doing it better than anyone else. She had never been surrounded by four grown men determined to punish a young man who was growing too big for his britches.

Which wasn't to say he didn't see the small abuses her stepfather attempted to visit upon her. Every few months, a rumor would surface that Rafael had brainwashed his wife or that she was heavily medicated or otherwise incapable of making her own decisions. Humbolt sold her favorite car "because it had become a liability" and forced her to fly in for meetings that were canceled at the last minute.

Rafael always retaliated. He paid for renovations at her summerhouse in Martha's Vineyard, closing it the week before her parents were scheduled to use it. He insisted they ship a number of rare paintings to their home in Athens and had his accounting team continually put pressure on Humbolt for financial reports that Alexandra didn't need.

It was tit-for-tat nonsense that didn't seem serious enough to get under Alexandra's skin as far as it did, but he didn't complain since her hatred of her parents made her as determined as he was to conquer and rule all corners of the world.

For the most part she managed her own money, but she frequently invested large chunks with him that he used for acquisitions and expansions, typically doubling her money before he rolled it back to her.

Meanwhile, she protected and assisted him in his endeavors by keeping her ears open. She would caution, "I've heard there's bad blood there. Cover yourself if you get into bed with them." Or, "Her father is in oil, if that interests you. We could invite her family onto the yacht."

The *Alexandra* was a forty-meter superyacht that he purchased when Alexandra had heard a rumor that a lesser royal was in trouble and needed a quiet bailing out. Rafael bought it for a third of its true value and regularly leased it out so it paid for itself. It had become not only a jewel in his corporate crown, but an excellent means of conducting business in a relaxed setting.

They had it to themselves on their first anniversary—with a full crew, obviously. Neither of them could be bothered to do more than carry a used cup to a sideboard for a refill, but they had no guests and thus were entertaining each other in their very favorite way.

Tonight, Alexandra was on her knees between his feet where he sat on the bed. She was curling his toes as she drew out his pleasure with tantalizing slowness, lavishing attention on his throbbing erection, humming with pleasure as she anointed him.

He watched as long as he could, fighting to hold on to his control. As much as he adored this act, however, he far preferred to hold back and prove to both of them that he was his own master, not her.

"Stop," he commanded in a voice that was so thick, it barely emerged from his throat.

She lifted her head, eyelids swollen, lips lax, the picture of eroticism.

"Are you not enjoying this, darling?" She blew softly on his wet flesh, causing his balls to tighten. The root of his shaft pulsed in her fist and he nearly finished from that alone.

"I want to be inside you." He lay back in a silent command for her to straddle him.

"Are you sure?" She pressed her fist down, drawing his skin taut as she painted a flagrant pattern with her tongue, tracing the shape of his tip. The dance of her tongue in the most exquisite place was his defeat.

With a guttural shout, he caught the worst of it in his palm, spilling the rest onto his belly, but as delicious as that orgasm was, he was irritated that she'd got the better of him.

She kissed the back of his hand and purred, "Such a gentleman."

She rose and walked away, still wearing the bra and garters and hose and five-inch heels that had brought him to attention before she'd tantalized him past his point of no return.

She returned with a warm damp cloth and cleaned him up with tender care.

His heart was still unsteady, his blood sizzling. He was so sexually gratified, he shouldn't be taking issue with the smug curl at the corners of her mouth, but he did. He felt... not weak, exactly, but not as superior as he liked to be.

Not that he wanted to lord over her. It wasn't like that between them. He had a lot of regard for this woman who wore tantalizing lingerie purely for his pleasure. The demi-cups of her bra were low enough to reveal her areoles, and the front of the thong barely covered her landing strip. Eyeing that peek and tease outfit was already causing him to twitch back to life.

She slipped out of her shoes and sprawled alongside him, warm and soft. Her hair fell around his face as she kissed him with the sort of passion most men dreamed of experiencing just once. He steeped himself in her constantly, basking in the fact that she was all his.

Yet she wasn't. *That* was the piece that was unsettling him. In this year of marriage, he had become deeply invested in their partnership. Sometimes he wondered if he was more invested than she was. He wasn't sure why he had that impression, but it had something to do with the way she drew firm boundaries around parts of herself and her past.

He wanted to know this was more than what it had been when they started, which was a combination of a very delicious affair and a very advantageous business arrangement. It should be a relief to him that their hearts weren't inextricably entangled, but he wanted a deeper commitment from her, something that cemented her place in his life.

"We should talk about children," he said when her lips slid to nibble at his jaw.

"Whose?" she asked, playing obtuse.

"Ours," he clarified.

"Right now?" Her tone lilted with disbelief.

"Soon," he deferred, recognizing he'd blindsided her and was losing more than the mood. Shadows of withdrawal had cooled the heat in her blue eyes. That was the exact opposite of what he was after.

He rolled so she was beneath him and set about returning the pleasure she'd given him tenfold. It took a few drawn out kisses for her to catch up, but then her desire reignited and she surpassed him, becoming frantic. When he ran his tongue beneath that thin strip of lace between her thighs, her hand fisted in his hair.

He loved when she was like this, clawing at him as though she couldn't get enough of him. He was both cruel and generous, insisting on taking her over the edge more than once before he finally entered her. By then, her lingerie was nothing but torn wrapping paper off an elegant gift, discarded on the floor, while she was naked and arching with abandon, welcoming his every thrust.

It was raw and rough and maybe imbued with his own desperation to bind them indelibly. It was also powerful, culminating in the sort of supernova climax that had her screaming and him shuddering in a paroxysm of ecstasy that damned near destroyed him.

In the aftermath, they were puddles of quivering flesh, exhausted. He barely had the energy to touch the button that doused the lights or drape his arm across her waist to spoon her into him.

He was roused some indeterminate time later, aware she was trying to leave the bed.

"Where are you going?" he asked through his desire to remain asleep.

"Nowhere," she murmured.

He thought he heard her sniff. It yanked him to a higher level of consciousness.

"Are you crying?"

"No. I have an eyelash in my eye. It's gone now. Go back to sleep."

He had a fleeting thought to turn on the light, but she snuggled her bottom into him and sighed, relaxing. He closed his eyes and drifted off again.

I can't lose him, Sasha thought as she stared into the dark.

Rafael's arm was heavy on her waist, but no matter how deeply asleep he was, he always noticed when she left the bed.

She had been weeping silently, afraid she would wake him, but putting physical space between them was next to impossible when lying against him was exactly where she wanted to be for the rest of her life.

Because she loved him? She was trying not to label it. That would give him even more influence over her than he already had. She was very careful to keep parts of herself back, pushing a persona of a spoiled heiress, an extrovert who loved to hostess, and a devoted if emotionally aloof wife.

She *was* devoted. She loved those moments when she made an introduction that clicked for him, or when her ability to charm a tycoon's wife smoothed the way for their husbands to strike a deal.

She loved being everything he needed because he was pretty much all she needed. She could survive without him; she knew she could. She had done it for years, but that's all she'd been doing: surviving. They had been long, lonely years filled with empty conversations at boring events with people who failed to interest her.

With Rafael, she thrived. They challenged each other and made each other laugh. He tapped into her stores of creativity, whether it was formulating a social strategy or designing their dream home. He gave her sensual pleasure that was like a drug, it was so intense and addictive.

Now he wanted a baby. She didn't ask why. It didn't matter why. If he wanted one, she had to decide whether to give him one or leave, because he had made clear from the beginning that this day would come.

She wanted to give him a baby. She wanted one for herself, but here came the tears again, welling up like blood from a wound.

She clenched her eyes shut, fighting the sobs that wanted to rack her body. Her lashes grew wet anyway and pressure built in her throat.

Her longing for a baby was so intense, it nearly stopped her heart, but it came with old and new yearnings. Hope and grief. Conflict.

Should she tell him?

No. Everything in her clenched up at the thought. There was too much shame in her, not for having a baby as a teenager and not even for placing her daughter with a loving family. On the contrary, she believed she had done the best thing for her daughter. At sixteen, she hadn't been ready to become a mother. Raising that baby with her mother and Humbolt would have been abuse, plain and simple.

Instead, she had done everything she could to provide a good life for her child, leaving her with a mother and a girl she had regarded as a sister. She was envious of the life she'd given her daughter.

No, her shame stemmed from how her baby had been conceived. Logically, Sasha knew that a married man of thirty who seduced a teenager was a predator, but it hadn't seemed like assault at the time. She'd been certain she knew what she was doing. It had been mischief. Something she had imagined throwing in Humbolt's face at some point.

As with all teenage rebellion, she'd been hideously naive to the consequences. She'd been four months pregnant before she had even begun to suspect it. By then, Humbolt had figured out who she was seeing. He blamed the affair on her. He knew which side his bread was buttered on and had been determined to protect his associate. *She* had tempted a married man, he said, calling her all sorts of horrific things. Did she want to destroy innocent lives? What of the man's wife and children? Had she thought about anyone but herself?

She hadn't, of course.

"Never tell your mother," Humbolt had warned. At first, she'd been too upset to even think of doing so. Later, she'd been under a legal obligation to bite her tongue, but her

mother had suspected the affair. That's why she had begun suggesting Sasha go back to school early.

By the time Sasha was sitting in a teen clinic in a rural part of New Jersey, having come as far away from Manhattan as she could get in hopes she wouldn't be recognized, she had known she was very much on her own.

Patricia Brooks, a midwife and reproductive counselor, had become her angel. She was the first person in Sasha's life to treat her as a person. Not an heiress who deserved a deferential attitude. Not a daughter, or stepdaughter, to be criticized and controlled. Not a sexualized body to be objectified, but a human being who could make decisions for herself.

Patty had laid out all of Sasha's choices, none of them without drawbacks.

"I have a duty to report if there's abuse," Patty had also said. "If the father is that much older than you…"

"If you tell anyone, I'll run away. I swear I will. My parents can't know I'm pregnant."

If she'd been an adult and having a baby, Sasha could have used the circumstance to take control of her trust, but having the baby while she was still a minor only created two people Humbolt would use for his own ends. Her baby would become another point of leverage Humbolt could use against her.

Termination was still on the table, barely, but Sasha had wanted to have the baby. In some ways, it had been the ultimate act of autonomy, exercising that monumental decision all by herself, but it was also love—not that she fully understood that emotion. Given her upbringing, it had been more of an attachment to the idea of love, but she'd felt something toward the baby that was bigger than anything she'd ever felt before.

On her third visit with Patty, when she told her that she wanted to have the baby, but couldn't raise it and didn't have anywhere to stay while she waited out her pregnancy, Patty invited her to live with her. She had a daughter at home of a similar age. She couldn't imagine Molly being in dire straits like this without anyone trustworthy to turn to.

Patty was risking her midwife practice by sheltering Sasha, but she was the calm, sensible counsel Sasha needed at the time. She helped her find a lawyer who handled asking the father to relinquish paternity. That was necessary for adoption, but Sasha refused to let him off without consequences of his own. She demanded an enormous trust be set up for her baby and didn't give a damn how he explained it to his wife.

He had gone along with it to "make the problem go away." His only stipulation was that Sasha couldn't tell anyone that he was the father, not even their child. Sasha was fine with that. She didn't need him. She had Patty.

And Molly.

At first, Patty's teenage daughter had been a bit of a pill, not sure what to think of this pregnant stranger who had moved into their spare bedroom, but over the ensuing months, they became as close as sisters. Or at least, the kind of sister Sasha had always wished she'd had.

In those days of homeschooling online and learning to cook and never caring about makeup or hair color or what she was wearing, Alexandra became herself. Sasha. She laughed at silly things and took nature walks like a country bumpkin and she grew a baby she loved in the way Patty loved Molly. In the way the two of them loved her.

Sasha could genuinely say it was the happiest time of her life—until she went into labor. That had been horrible, but thankfully quick and uncomplicated.

Then she was holding a tiny girl who looked too small for a long name like Elizabeth, which was the name she'd chosen.

Molly said, "You could call her Libby," and that's who she became.

If she could, Sasha would have lived with them forever and raised her daughter there, but her mother was finally suspecting she wasn't in Ibiza. Staying here would risk all the careful precautions she'd taken to hide that she'd had a baby at all.

"I have to leave, but I can't bring her with me," she told Patty when her daughter was a week old. "I *can't*."

"But—" Molly protested.

They were close enough by then that Sasha knew what was bothering her friend. Molly had said it once before.

"How will you leave your baby with strangers?"

"If you're absolutely certain this is what you want," Patty said carefully, "then I wonder if you'll consider letting me adopt her? It could be an open adoption," Patty rushed on. "That way you could check up on her and see her anytime."

Such profound relief washed through her, Sasha barely heard Molly say a quietly ecstatic, "Really, Mom?"

"You can never tell anyone, Moll," Sasha warned her. "Ever. I mean that."

"I know," Molly said solemnly. "I swear I never will."

Three days later, Sasha signed the papers and walked away from her baby, confident she was leaving Libby with people who would give her a far better life and infinitely more love than she could.

It broke her heart. It left her numb for a year or more, uncaring that Humbolt had her assessed by a counselor who diagnosed her as having used toxic drugs. She'd gone to rehab meetings for months, never telling the counselor the real reason she was disassociated and depressed.

Eventually, she rallied enough to go back to school. She returned to ski holidays and attending film premiers and, pretty soon, she had almost convinced herself that it had simply been a very weird dream. It hadn't really happened.

It had, though. She was already a mother.

And she couldn't bring herself to tell Rafael. Keeping Libby hidden was as much for her daughter's protection as her own. Even if he were to find out at this late stage, Humbolt could cause a lot of damage to Libby's life. To Patty's. He would do his best to ruin Patty's career, possibly try to have her arrested.

What would that do to Libby? To all of them?

No. Sasha couldn't expose them to any of that. She would hold on to her secret until she was in her grave or Humbolt was in his.

In the meantime, she would have a baby with Rafael. This time she would keep her baby and everything would be perfect and wonderful.

She finally fell asleep, waking late and finding Rafael on deck, already finished with his breakfast and nursing his second cup of coffee.

"I left you sleeping, thinking you needed it. You were restless last night." He searched her gaze.

"Too much champagne," she said with a breezy shrug. "Good thing I got that out of my system since I won't be allowed alcohol if we're trying for a baby."

"Really?" A light came into his gaze that made her heart flip over. "You want to?"

"I do." Her insides were vibrating as she let him draw her from her chair into his lap, never dreaming in that moment that *try* would become such a loaded, painful word.

CHAPTER FOUR

Fourteen months later...

After months of cajoling, Rafael had finally got Gio Casella onto his yacht.

Gio was his contemporary in age, but old, old money from Genoa, Italy. He ran a sprawling, well-established global conglomerate, Casella Corp. Hammering out a deal with him would go a long way to finally proving Rafael had as much right to ply international shipping waters as anyone else.

Gio was not, however, interested in the female company Alexandra had arranged for him.

Jacinda was the niece of someone moderately important from somewhere vaguely notable. Alexandra knew her from her boarding school days. Jacinda was beautiful and well-mannered, but a little too blatant in her attempt to earn Gio's favor. She had taken off her top as she entered the pool, and her breasts were definitely lovely, but she was practically rubbing them all over Gio, which Rafael suspected from Gio's indifference was actually more irritating than tantalizing.

Perhaps a swim after lunch had been a bad idea. Rafael should have suggested they get back to business, but

Alexandra had been tasked with entertaining the rest of their guests all morning. He'd brought Gio out to the lido deck hoping a relaxing drink would keep everyone sociable and happy.

Alexandra had her own top off, all the women did, but even though she was lying on a lounger, she didn't seem to be relaxed. She'd been off her game when she assembled this particular crowd, misjudging Gio's bachelor status as a man looking for a good time. Rafael couldn't take her to task for it. She had been going through a lot. It was distracting her and causing fissures in their relationship.

A week ago, as they'd been preparing for this trip, she'd got her period. Again.

"Perhaps we should consider other options," he'd said when she had announced that with her usual *discussion over* tone.

"We're running out of options, aren't we?" she'd snapped.

That had been the third round of IVF so she wasn't wrong.

"Look, I know you're disappointed, but—" he began.

"Don't tell me what I feel." Her mood went from ice to explosive in a millisecond, leaving her shaking and teary as she glared at him. "Don't tell me this is okay. This is something my body should be able to *do*, Rafael."

"*I* want to quit trying while we reassess," he said firmly, making that decision for both of them. "We could both use a break from the pressure."

"Oh, could you? Do you need a break from filling a cup once in a while?" she asked, voice pitched to the height of resentment.

He clenched his teeth against engaging. Whatever frustration he was suffering, she was going through worse. He knew that. Injections and procedures and waiting, only to find it hadn't worked.

But he stuck by his decision. When they came aboard, he brought her a glass of wine, which she accepted with an air of resignation.

Since then, she had been drinking freely, not getting sloppy, but acting more the life of the party, the way she had in their early days. She trotted out salacious stories from "before my husband tamed me," and flirted outrageously with him, leaning to show him her cleavage and gripping the inside of his thigh over dinner.

Rafael didn't mind. Whenever she teased him in front of an audience, she always came through behind doors. He dismissed it as her blowing off steam from their latest disappointment, but he realized her infertility was affecting her far more deeply than she was letting on.

He *hated* that she took her body's inability to get pregnant as a personal failure. It was bad luck and he was genuinely saddened by it, but he couldn't say so. Anytime he tried to talk about it, she shut things down with the swiftness of a guillotine blade.

He was also off his game, he admitted to himself as he stepped behind the bar to make martinis. He was hoping another round of drinks would relax his wife and loosen up Gio, but he was probably better off asking the man to head back to the negotiating table.

As the suggestion formed on his lips, his purser arrived with an unfamiliar young woman. She wasn't part of the crew and reminded him vaguely of someone who might show him to a table at a streetside bistro. She wore a simple cotton blouse over wide-legged pants and mass-made sandals. She held a leather portfolio and her skimming glance locked on Gio where he lounged in the pool.

Gio had mentioned something about bringing two assistants aboard so unrelated work could continue while he negotiated with Rafael. Rafael had assented and forgotten about it.

He would have dismissed the interruption as completely unimportant but his wife hissed with unmistakable enmity, "What are you doing here?"

The poor woman was taken aback and looked like a shopgirl getting a dressing down over not having a requested size in stock.

It wasn't like Alexandra to be openly rude to anyone except her parents. She typically used honey, not vinegar, especially with staff. Was she still angry that he'd suggested they take a break from trying for a baby, and taking it out on this stranger?

"What's wrong, Alexandra?" Jacinda said from her position beside Gio in the pool. "Is the help supposed to stay belowstairs? You're such a snob."

"Molly is my assistant's assistant," Gio said crisply. "What do you need, Molly?"

"Valentina…um…" She waved the portfolio, looking pale at having been put on the spot. "She said you wanted to sign this as soon as it was ready."

"Your executive assistant has an assistant?" Rafael drawled, trying to defuse the tension that charged the air like electricity. "No wonder it was so difficult to get hold of you to extend this invitation."

He shot a look at Alexandra. She knew how important Gio was to solidifying the trade and cargo arm of the Zamos Corp.

Alexandra was shoving her arms into her cover-up, pushing her sunglasses onto her nose, and dropping a sun hat over her hair, but her mouth was tight with dismay.

Gio said something and left the pool so Molly could bring the portfolio to him.

Rafael wasn't really tracking the pair, too busy watching his wife as he finished shaking the martinis, then poured them out. When he took one to Alexandra, she said, "Thank you, my love," and took a big gulp. A *big* one.

What the hell was going on?

He glanced toward Molly. She was handing a pen to Gio, her back stiff as a board.

Rafael felt some compassion for her. He'd been on the receiving end of a "you don't belong here" fugue many times himself.

Gio signed the document and looked to Rafael. "I'd like this in London by morning."

"Of course." Rafael nodded at the purser to make it happen.

"I'm very sorry," Molly murmured, seeming cowed. "I'll stay below from now on."

"I was just surprised." Alexandra was on the defensive, finally catching up to how poorly she was behaving. "I'm usually informed when guests bring staff aboard."

"You thought we had a stowaway?" Rafael sipped his glass of icy gin, still thinking she was acting grossly out of character.

"What exactly do you do for Gio?" Alexandra asked Molly, finally dredging up the charming woman he was more familiar with, the one who showed everyone polite interest and effortlessly smoothed over social hiccups. She asked about Molly's duties, then wound up overcompensating by inviting the woman to breakfast. *What the hell?*

Molly agreed and left. A short while later, Rafael and Gio dressed and retreated to the office, where they continued discussing their potential partnership.

Rafael was still distracted, though. With his business thriving and this deal looking as though it would go through, he should be feeling more confident than ever, but he kept thinking about how the desire for children was eroding his marriage. Alexandra was suffering. He couldn't ignore that, nor did he know how to fix it. The whole thing filled him with a painful, nagging helplessness—which was the worst feeling in the world for him.

What the hell was he going to do?

Her past was catching up to her. Sasha could hear it like hounds in the distance, yelping and howling as they pursued her.

She hugged her silk kimono against the breeze coming through the open doors to the deck off their stateroom. It wasn't a cold wind. After growing up in New York and schooling in Switzerland, she rarely allowed herself to suffer anything below a balmy seventy degrees. That's why she had married a Greek and settled with him in Athens.

That's why she had persuaded him to sail them south, so she could feel these hot, dry winds off Africa, hoping they would dispel the chill of harsh reality that seemed determined to take residence in her bones.

"I was plan—"

Sasha jolted when Rafael's hand touched her shoulder and his voice resounded behind her ear.

"Did you not hear me in the shower?" he asked in an

amused rumble. He folded his arms around her as an apology for startling her, drawing her back into his naked chest.

In moments like this, when his hard arms were around her, she felt safe and cherished and almost believed they would be okay.

"I was just thinking," she murmured, letting herself melt into his humid, near-naked frame.

"About?" His prompt was a warm vibration against her back.

About how angry she was with her body. How she felt as though these fertility problems were her fault. That this was some sort of karmic punishment.

It wasn't. Not exactly. Endometriosis happened to women who hadn't already carried a baby. There was no known cause. They only knew that it got worse with time. Perhaps if she'd tried to become pregnant sooner, she would have had a better outcome, but she hadn't. How could she have known? Her symptoms hadn't been bad enough for her to know a fertility problem was developing.

When she didn't answer him, Rafael rubbed her upper arms and said, "I'll call off your meeting."

"What? Why?" She stepped out of his arms and turned to confront him. He could be so overbearing sometimes!

And damn him for being built like a god. He wore only the fluffy white towel that barely clung to his hips. She was accosted by his naked chest, each muscle delineated to perfection. Her very favorite thing was to kiss the planes and subtle dips of his shoulders and chest and biceps and throat, where she could make him swallow simply by looking there.

"You got a little loose last night." His wide hand cupped

the side of her neck. "I'm not complaining. *At all*. But you should sleep in."

Her cheeks stung and she couldn't bring herself to lift her gaze to his smug smile or the gratification in his gaze. She'd been all over him last night. She had played it off as being tipsy, but it had been more than that. Desperation had driven her to rub and writhe and take him in her mouth. To sob and encourage him to take her deeper. Faster. *Harder*.

So much of their lovemaking seemed to be driven by desperation these days, as though they both sensed how close they were to being rent apart.

Maybe it was just her that felt that way, though.

"What's going on?" His thumb tilted her jaw upward, gently insisting she look at him. His expression had turned grave. "Regret?"

"For last night? Of course not." That was true, but other things? Oh, yes. She had so many regrets, she was drowning in them.

It was causing the veil between Sasha and Alexandra to slip, which terrified her. Alexandra was the strong woman she wanted to be. The one who didn't suffer fools or heartaches and was impervious to the cruel impacts of life.

Sasha was tortured and needy and yearned for love. She *hurt*. All the time.

She did what always worked when she was agitated and feeling defenseless around him. She reached for *his* veil, the edge of the towel he wore, plucking it loose while boldly holding his gaze.

"Did I sound like I was suffering regrets last night?" she challenged.

His lips parted to say something, but his breath turned to a hiss as she dropped the towel and caressed his hardening flesh. Something flashed behind his eyes. Suspicion? He knew she was trying to distract him.

She licked her lips suggestively and started to sink to her knees.

"No." His voice was gruff. He took hold of her arms, stopping her. "I was rough with you last night. Let me kiss it and make it better." He dragged her against him and the heat of his body penetrated the thin silk of the kimono, stealing her ability to speak. His hand fisted in her loose hair and tugged her head back so he could capture her mouth with his own, kissing her long and deep.

She splayed her hands on his naked skin, instantly overwhelmed. Distantly, she knew she ought to catch herself back from the rush of desire, from the way she so easily capitulated to him, but her hands roamed all over his back and buttocks, trying to touch all of him. Trying to incite him. Trying to be the one in charge.

He did the same, but with greater effect. His slow hand rubbed silk against her skin, conveying that she could become as frantic as she wanted, but he was in no hurry. Not today.

"D-don't you have people waiting for you?" she asked breathlessly, when he slid his lazy kisses into the crook of her neck.

"They can wait."

This, too, was her downfall. He made her feel special. He made her feel as though she was his priority. The only thing that was important to him.

She desperately needed that right now.

She lifted her arms to curl around his neck, but he stopped her so he could tug open her kimono. His gaze dropped to admire and caress her breasts.

"Are your nipples sore? I'll be gentle." He bent to lick one, leaving it wet and tightening as the breeze from the open door washed across it. "I thought we had both used up our capacity for sexual hunger last night." He cupped and weighed her breast in his hot palm. "But I'm suddenly starving. Are you sure you want this?"

"Always," she admitted on a pang of distress, then rallied, trying to save face. "Why? Afraid you can't keep up with me?"

She tightened her arms around his neck, trying to mash herself against him. She felt him stiffen before he made a noise that was a scoff and a scold.

"*Glikia mou*, you know your pleasure is my pleasure. I'll always deliver as much as I possibly can." He scooped her up, so her legs instinctually wrapped his waist. "Until you beg me to stop."

As he took a few steps, his erection shifted against the naked flesh that was still tender from their energetic love-making last night.

Then she was falling, clasping in panic, but he was catching her before setting her on the settee that ran beneath the windows.

One lingering kiss on her lips was all he gave her before he knelt and arranged her so he could bend and anoint her most intimate flesh. He rubbed his freshly shaved cheeks against her inner thighs and blew softly on her sensitized mound and tasted her in a lazy and oh, so tender fashion.

"Rafael," she moaned.

"What do you need, *louloudi mou*? Stop?"

"No," she moaned, feeling as though she would burst. "Please don't stop."

He growled out a noise of satisfaction and set to pleasuring her, refusing to rush, making her arch and sob and dig her heel into his back.

It was infuriating to be this helpless to him, but it was such a wondrous trap to be held in. When they were like this, all her anguish and regret fell away. She was nothing but a single point of pleasure, needing nothing beyond the continuation of these incredible ripples of sensation.

There was something lonely and solitary in this particular moment, though. She wanted him to be as caught up as she was, thrusting into her with abandon. The longer he pleasured her, the more she felt herself slipping away. He was stealing pieces of her soul, one by one.

"I want you inside me." She caught a handful of his hair, but he only hugged her thighs in his strong arms and pressed his tongue to that bundle of nerves, so swollen and throbbing.

Climax twisted through her abdomen. A ball of joy detonated within her, sending shock waves of ecstasy through her limbs.

He lightened up, but didn't let up, continuing to pleasure her through the peak and into the trembling aftermath.

Her belly was still quivering and her heart rate still uneven when he rose to stand over her, fully hard with arousal, gaze taking in her helpless sprawl.

She didn't even have the strength to reach out and grip him in her fist, but he didn't seem to expect it. He trailed his fingers from her navel to run a caressing knuckle along the underside of her breast, then brushed a tendril of hair from her cheek.

"Thank you. I enjoyed that." He bent to retrieve his towel.

A sob of disbelief hit her throat. "Don't you want to…?" *Take me.*

"Later. Gio is expecting me." He slid a glance to the clock on the night table as he rewrapped the towel around his hips. "I'll cancel your breakfast meeting so you can sleep."

"No." She sat up, mind still scattered.

"Why not? It's not important."

He said it very casually, but the full weight of his attention zeroed in on her.

Oh, you bastard, she thought.

This whole thing was a deliberate attempt to disconcert her. Which she would have found contemptible if she hadn't tried it first and *failed*.

"I need something to think about beyond my own inadequacy." She stood to retie her kimono.

"Stop that," he ordered. "It's not helpful to blame yourself. *I* don't blame you."

"Goodness, if *you* don't blame me, then I shouldn't dare, should I?" She knew that would get a rise out of him. That's why she'd said it.

They glared at one another, turning into the worst pair of bickering fools. If she had seen anyone else behaving this way, she would have said, *Get a divorce, already.*

The thought sent ice tumbling through her, chilling her bones.

"No," he said grimly. "You shouldn't." He walked into the bathroom where she heard water begin to run.

So arrogant. And yet he was trying to be supportive in his way. He didn't know, though. He didn't know why she was so angry with herself.

Tell him.

Then what? What if he looked at her with the same contempt Humbolt had shown? With the same contempt she felt for herself? She couldn't take that. She really couldn't.

He walked into the closet so she went into the bathroom where she hung her kimono and stepped into the shower.

By the time she came out, he was gone.

CHAPTER FIVE

"MOLLY. THANK YOU for coming." Sasha used the lofty tone her mother would use when welcoming a decorator or some other contracted person into her home. She let her into the stateroom, then glanced up and down the empty corridor before closing the door.

When she faced Molly, she found her old friend turning a slow circle in the middle of the lounge. The suite was enormous, with a bookshelf as a partition between the parlor and the bedroom, then a private deck in the bow.

Molly's brunette hair was in a tidy bun, her pantsuit off-the-rack. She was still a bit of a country girl with her eyes agog and her jaw slack, but she was also Molly, so her heart was on full display.

"I am *so sorry*." Her expression crumpled into anxiety as she faced Sasha. "I had no idea you were Alexandra Zamos. I wouldn't have come. I certainly wouldn't have shown up on the lido deck! I won't say a word, Sash." Her voice was barely above a whisper. *"I swear."*

Sit down. Let's eat. That's what Sasha had planned to say to her, before she asked Molly how much money she wanted to keep her trap shut.

Instead, she found herself rushing forward and throwing her arms around her.

Molly released a small "eep" of surprise before she hugged her back. They were no longer adolescent girls. It made their hug unfamiliar yet still a homecoming. The acceptance in it was water on Sasha's parched soul.

"It's so good to see you," Molly said.

It's good to see you, too.

That's what Sasha wanted to say, but she was starting to cry.

How embarrassing. She hadn't fallen apart like that in years. Maybe ever.

Oh, she cried every time she got her period, but with anger, cutting short her pity party as quickly as she could, then swiping away her tears with resentment.

This had been a release of emotions she had bottled the day she'd walked away from Molly's home in New Jersey. From her baby and the only other two people in this world she loved with all her heart.

Sasha washed her face and came out with a cold facecloth that she continued to dab against her eyes, hoping to reduce the swelling and redness before Rafael returned.

"Sit. Eat. Please," she said with an impatient wave toward the table when she saw Molly was still hovering. "How's your mom?"

"Good. We're all good." Molly sat, but her eyes were red from shared tears and she pressed a tissue beneath her nose before looking at Sasha with an earnest expression that searched hers while shining with expectation of some kind. "Libby is wonderful, Sash. She's so smart and funny. Sometimes she asks about y—"

"Don't," she choked, feeling as though she'd been stabbed in the chest. "I can't hear about her, Molly. I can't."

Especially now, when she knew Libby was the only baby she was likely to ever carry.

Such longing gripped her, she could barely breathe. Tears rose hotly in her eyes again.

In an attempt to regain her composure, she sat to pour their coffee, thinking her mother was good for something, having taught her to ignore difficult displays of emotion and pretend all was well.

She had to explain, though. "Rafael doesn't know. I've never told anyone. It has to stay that way."

Molly's silence was thick with hurt. When she spoke, however, her voice was stiff with indignation. "I understand and respect that, but I won't pretend my sister doesn't exist."

And that right there, that mixture of compassion for her, with fierce pride and defense of the child she called her sister, told Sasha she had made the right decision leaving her baby with Patty and Molly.

"Can I ask how you met Rafael?"

Sasha leaped on telling that story, painting a full picture of how gorgeous he'd been in his tuxedo, how he'd asked her to dance and she'd felt as though she was in a dream.

"All under the nose of some knob my parents wanted me to marry."

Molly lifted an amused look from her poached egg and smoked salmon on a toasted crostini. She was so refreshing. Molly didn't fuss around with diets or hair color or push-up bras. *Her* mother had taught her that if a man didn't love you as you were, then he didn't love *you*.

Sasha had always envied her that confidence in her own self-worth.

She finished out the story with the secret elopement and dramatic announcement over brunch. She almost added,

Libby's father was there, but she shied away from that part of it. It had been enough to throw her new husband in his face.

"It sounds like love at first sight," Molly said with a wistful smile.

Sasha's cup hit her saucer with a loud clank.

"We agreed from the beginning that we were using each other to some extent. In a practical way, I mean. Not cold-hearted. Our feelings have grown over time." It wasn't dishonest to say that, but she didn't want to admit to anyone, including herself, how uneven the emotional investment was between herself and her husband. "Rafael indulges me, which I can't say I hate." Even if she wished his "darlings" and other endearments were more sincere. "He's caring and supportive." In his way.

It's not helpful to blame yourself.

"We have each other's respect, which is more than I expected to have with any man." Mostly. She recalled his assertion of control this morning and grew pensive, then insisted brightly, "The sex is fantastic." She offered a wicked grin, ignoring the ache of loneliness that had been sitting like a block of ice in her middle for the longest time.

"I'm happy for you, Sash." Molly wasn't exactly gushing, though. She was trying to peer past the veneer of nonchalance that Sasha wore.

"What about you?" Sasha turned the tables. "Anyone special in your life?"

"No." Molly's cheeks went pink as she reached for her coffee. "I'm focused on my career."

"You mean your boss?" Sasha teased.

"Oh, my God. *Please* tell me it's not obvious?" she begged with mortification.

"I was almost catatonic with shock yesterday, but I could still tell there was something between you. Are you seeing him?"

"God no! He doesn't even know I'm alive."

Sasha's radar had picked up something else, but she kept it to herself. She knew how people at Gio's level operated. A few short years ago, he had nearly married a woman who had noble roots, a vineyard in Tuscany, and a château in the south of France. Molly was far more special than any of those things, but a rich prat like Gio might be oblivious to it and see only a pretty woman with a crush that he could use for his own ends.

"I can't help being attracted to him," Molly confided with a cringe of helplessness. "You saw him."

"I only have eyes for my husband," Sasha insisted, but she wasn't dead. Gio Casella was definitely a looker. "Promise me you won't let him play you like a flute."

"Don't worry. It's never going to happen. I wouldn't know what to do if it did. I can't imagine being involved with someone who lives like this." Molly glanced around. "I'm glad you're happy, though."

Me, too, Sasha tried to say, but had to bite her lip because it was starting to quiver. The raw, septic wound in her heart burst open and the words flowed out.

"I can't get pregnant."

"What?" Molly sat up straighter, then reached across to squeeze her hand. "It can take a long time for some people, Sash. Don't lose hope. Do you want to call Mom? She might be able to help." She looked for her phone.

"It's been a year and a half." Which was nothing. She knew there were people who tried for a decade before they saw results, but Rafael had insisted they take a break and that terrified her. If she couldn't give him a baby, would he still want *her*?

"I'm seeing specialists and we've tried IVF *three* times." Sasha picked up the damp cloth to press it against the salty tears beginning to burn the edges of her eyelids again. "We both want a baby, but my body won't work and it's so unfair, Moll. I did this once before. I should be able to do it again." The resentment was rising like a tide, pushing the tears into her eyes and nose and throat. "And I keep thinking it's my fault that—"

"No. Sasha, *no*." Molly reached to crush her hand in her two warm ones. "Talk to Mom. She'll tell you there are a thousand reasons a woman might have trouble conceiving. None of them are your fault. But you also know that if you want to be in Libby's life, we would love for you—"

"No. Molly." She snatched her hand away and shifted sideways in her chair, clutching where her chest was still cleaved in half by that long-ago loss. "Rafael wants an heir of his own. Not… I mean, we've talked a little about adoption, but he's adopted. I can tell there's a part of him that wants a blood connection, you know? I want that, too. I want *our* baby and I'm so angry with myself that I can't give him this."

"Is *he* angry?" Molly's voice hardened. "Is he putting pressure on you?"

"No." She dashed at the tears that were overflowing her lashes. "He said we should take a break from trying, which makes me feel like even more of a failure."

"Oh, Sasha." Molly started to come around to hug her, but Sasha brushed her off.

"You'll make me cry again." She picked up the soggy cloth and pressed it to her eyes.

"Take that down and look at me."

She didn't want to, but Molly sounded so much like Patty with that firm tone of tough love, she dropped the cloth into her lap.

Molly was crouched in front of her, somber. "A man twice your age took advantage of you. You didn't do anything wrong—"

"He was married, Molly. I knew it was wrong."

"You were *sixteen*. He was an adult. He said he loved you. He manipulated you and left you to deal with a pregnancy *alone*. Do not pretend your crime is equal to his. That's something Humbolt would do, and you know what a piece of garbage he is."

Sasha pushed the wet cloth against her eyes again, pressing back emotive tears. She was touched by the way Molly was still willing to be her champion.

It was true, though. She could still hear Humbolt calling her a slut and a homewrecker and some dark part of her continued to believe it.

"Have you ever talked to anyone? A counselor?" Molly was smoothing her hair the way her mother had done when Sasha had been so troubled, living with strangers, contemplating the biggest decision of her life.

"About him? Never. My fertility specialist recommended someone for the pregnancy troubles, but I'd have to tell them about all of that and…" She looked helplessly to Molly and her heart constricted with agony. "I can't. I can't talk to anyone about any of this. There's no one I trust. Rafael tries to understand, but he doesn't." And she didn't trust him—them—enough to reveal it to him.

"Talk to me, then. Get it off your chest." Molly moved back into her chair.

Sasha took a deep breath and breathed out all her hopelessness.

"It's endometriosis. Severe. I can keep trying until the cows come home, but I'll probably never get pregnant. I don't want to accept that, but I can't keep doing this with the shots and the exams and the procedures that fail. It's like having a miscarriage every time because I convince myself that I'm pregnant, then I'm not. And it makes me such a moody bitch I don't know how Rafael stays married to me." Her voice turned into a choke as the fear of her marriage ending ran through her like an electric current, hot and painful. "Why did I get pregnant by a man I hate, but I can't get pregnant by a man I love? It's so *unfair*, Moll."

"Oh, Sash. I'm so sorry." Molly's expression was agonized on her behalf.

For once, the weight of her sadness shifted slightly. It was no longer suffocating her. Molly was holding some of it for her and that made her want to hug her. How could she keep her in her life, she wondered? Yesterday, she had told Gio she wouldn't try to poach his assistant, but she would gladly pay Molly to be her friend again, just for this little bit of emotional support she offered her.

"Have you considered a surrogate?" Molly asked gently.

"Not seriously." Sasha sighed again. "I would have to tell people why I need one." Failure was inching back into her tight throat.

"You don't have to tell anyone anything. It's your business how you make a baby," Molly said with affront.

"We'd still have to interview people. Whoever we chose would be a stranger. It feels too invasive to let someone I don't know into our lives like that." She was greedy. Inse-cure, maybe, because she didn't want to share Rafael with someone she didn't know and trust. "That's why I want to do it myself, but I *can't*. And I'm so tired of being miser-able and useless and *alone*, Moll." Her eyes welled afresh, which just made her mad because tears were useless, too.

"Oh, Sasha, stop punishing yourself. I wish you'd let me tell you how happy you made us. I know that doesn't fix anything for you, but I wish you could be proud of what you gave us. If I could—" Molly bit her lips, apprehension coming into her face.

"What?" Sasha looked behind her, terrified that Rafael had walked in and overheard them, but the room was empty. "What?" she insisted to Molly.

"I needed to double-think what I was going to say," Molly said with a twitch of bemusement around her lips. Her brows gathered into a frown of gravity. "Because I don't want to say it unless I mean it, and I do. If I could give you the same happiness you gave us, I would, Sasha. What if I tried? What if I was your surrogate?"

Sasha's heart took a hard bounce.

"Moll." She made herself dismiss the offer because Molly was just being her kind and loyal and heart-forward self. Sasha hadn't known how to maintain their friendship without risking Libby, but she was sorry she had let so many years go by without speaking to her friend.

"I'm being serious." Molly leaned forward with the ear-nest, open warmth that filled Sasha with optimism that, somehow, things would work out. "I would need tests to see if it's feasible, but you know how badly I had always wanted a sister. You gave me one. I would argue that you gave me two, because I've never forgotten you." Her mouth widened with a sentimental smile. "And Libby has been such a gift, Sash. I can't even describe how much Mom and I love her. If I could give you someone to love that hard, then I want to."

"Molly, stop. How would I even explain it to Rafael? How—"

"'How' is a yes," Molly noted with her mother's clear logic. "You're saying you'll let me try. Aren't you?"

She shouldn't, but hope was making her latch on to the logistics, skipping right over whether allowing Molly to do this was wise.

But it would bring her friend back into her life. It would mean she didn't have to tell anyone—including Rafael—about her past because Molly already knew.

"It's too much for me to ask of you, Moll," Sasha protested weakly.

"You're not asking. I'm offering." A huge smile was breaking across her face. "Please let me try. I want to do this for you if I can, Sasha. I really do."

Sasha was speechless, unable to imagine how they would manage it or how she would repay her, but she jerkily nodded. "If you're sure, then yes. Please. Let's try."

"Do you have business in London soon?" Alexandra asked when they arrived at their villa in Attica, overlooking Dikastika Bay, about an hour from Athens.

Built to his wife's specifications, the house had more stairs than Rafael would have liked, given its five floors, but it was not only tasteful and the envy of any guest for its panoramic views, river stone pool, and xeriscape grounds, but it felt like a home. They casually shed their travel clothes and dipped naked into the water, confident their staff would busy themselves with unpacking and allow them their privacy.

"Nothing pressing, why?" He'd been away from the office for nearly two weeks and, while he was productive aboard the *Alexandra*, he had a lot to attend to at headquarters now that he was back, not least of which was following up on the fine points of the deal he'd negotiated with Gio Casella. Gio had a London office, though. Perhaps it would be useful to meet with him there.

"I think I've found us a surrogate."

"What?" He ducked and arrowed closer to her in a wide sweep of his arms, surfacing where she was treading water, but he could stand on the bottom of the pool. "How? *Who?*"

"You don't sound pleased." The blur of her naked body shifted as she also reached her foot toward the shallow end and stood on the bottom.

"You've never wanted to talk about a surrogate." Granted, that had been as they were going into the third IVF, but... "This seems like something we ought to discuss and decide together."

"We're discussing it now." She was being her loftiest, most irritatingly snooty self, barely looking at him as she turned her back and waded to the stairs.

She continued to be the most alluring woman he'd ever seen as she stepped naked under the outdoor shower, keeping her hair out of the water as she'd done in the pool. She rinsed, then turned off the spray before shaking out a bath sheet from the cupboard.

"Or not," she added as she wrapped the towel around herself, referring to his dumbfounded silence.

"Tell me, then." He came out behind her and snapped the shower on, blasting the water against his face and chest, turned to rinse his hair, then snapped it off and accepted the towel she handed him.

The evening was cool, but he didn't dry off. He wrapped the towel around his hips and followed her up the outer stairs to their bedroom.

The maid quickly excused herself and hurried from the room, leaving them to the long shadows of sunset while they dressed.

"You remember I had breakfast with Gio's assistant?" There was something in her voice that made his ears strain, certain there was more to hear in her tone than its deliberate casualness.

"Molly," he recollected.

"You remember her name?" Her head turned so she could sear him with her gaze.

"No need to be possessive, darling. Banking names is a useful skill."

"Hmph. Well, we got to talking about my issues."

"How?" It came out with unvarnished astonishment. "You never talk about it with anyone." She barely talked to him about it and had flatly refused to see a professional counselor, no matter how much he and their fertility specialist suggested it might be helpful.

"She mentioned her mother is a midwife." She shrugged. "It came out and, long story short, she offered to be our surrogate."

He choked on disbelief. *"Why?"* As if he didn't know.

"Are you really going to look down on someone who is willing to carry a pregnancy for money? You married me for mine," she reminded him.

"Touché." His reaction had been a reflex of his well-honed cynicism. He stepped into his trousers. "You're right.

It's labor." Literally. He'd never thought of it that way, but, "It deserves compensation."

"Is that what you think being my husband is? *Work?*" she asked with affront, head poking from the knitted top she pulled over it.

Damn, she was prickly these days.

"More of a calling, darling," he assured her, approaching to skim his hands alongside her neck, freeing her hair from the collar. "But I deserve danger pay sometimes."

He started to drop a kiss on her mouth, but she turned her face away, brows elevated to a piqued angle.

He kissed her cheekbone and testily turned away to search out his own shirt.

"What makes you think she's the right sort of person?" he asked as he threaded his arms into his sleeves. "Has she done it before?"

"No." She pulled on snug yoga pants. "She warned me that could be a roadblock. Doctors don't usually work with a surrogate who hasn't had a successful pregnancy of their own."

Rafael dismissed that. Nearly any roadblock could be overcome for a price.

"What makes you think she's right for the job?" For *us*?

"She's discreet."

"How do you know?"

"She wouldn't be working for Gio if she wasn't."

True.

"She seems conscientious and capable of restraint. I offered her a mimosa, but she refused. Said she was on the clock."

"High praise."

"Look, you know I don't trust easily. She seems honest

and responsible, plus she's stationed in London. Dr. Narula started her practice there. I imagine she still has good contacts to recommend. This saves me advertising my infertility to find someone else. I think it's worth exploring. At the very least, we should let her get tested to see if she's suitable. I won't get my hopes up until I know whether it's even possible."

Rafael's instincts were still prickling, telling him there was more going on here than she was revealing, but he was so damned relieved that she sounded optimistic for a change, he didn't want to ruin it by voicing misgivings. She was right. There was little harm in running the tests.

"If this is what you want, then fine. Find out if she's suitable."

"Really?" Finally, she turned to face him.

Alexandra was a sophisticated woman with a razor-sharp intelligence and a jaded sense of humor. She was so beautiful, she knocked the breath out of him and had from the first time he'd spied her across a room, but occasionally, like now, when her face was clean of makeup and her poise slipped to reveal how badly she wanted something, she looked very young and vulnerable.

It caused a dip and roll inside his chest, one that had always disturbed him, because that's not who they were. He relied on her to be as guarded and battle-ready as he was. Armed to the teeth.

Most of the time she was. The last thing he would call her was "maternal," but in this moment, he couldn't ignore how badly she wanted a baby. He wanted to give her a family in any way he could. If that meant hiring a surrogate, so be it.

"Yes," he said firmly, cupping her cheek and pressing his

mouth to hers, heartened when her cool hands arrived on his neck and her lips clung to his. "I want you to be happy, Alexandra. I've always wanted that." He had thought that was an easy assignment until the baby troubles arose. "If you think this will work, then proceed."

She curled her arms tighter around his neck, so her whole body was stretched against his and breathed a heartfelt, "Thank you," against his ear.

CHAPTER SIX

Between Christmas and travel and various tests, then the harvesting and fertilization of fresh eggs and mandatory counseling, it was April before implantation occurred.

Sasha had offered to stay in London with Molly while she waited out the result, but Molly was working. They were both aware that it might take several rounds before there was a successful implant. Molly had agreed to try three times, which Sasha thought was more than generous, considering how invasive and time consuming the procedure was.

So Sasha was with Rafael in Rio de Janeiro, eating breakfast on the terrace of their hotel room overlooking Copacabana Beach, when "Dr. Kala Narula" came up on her phone.

She stabbed to accept the call. Kala's assistant brought Molly onto the screen in a separate box, then Kala appeared.

"Good morning, Alexandra. Hello, Molly. Is Rafael here, too?" Kala asked.

"Yes." Sasha flashed a look to him and tightened her hand on the phone.

He set down his coffee, listening intently.

"Congratulations—"

Sasha's ears filled with water. She didn't hear the rest. Stinging waves of emotion rolled through her. Were they positive feelings? Negative? She didn't know. She only knew they made her heart race and her lungs search for oxygen. She couldn't see anything but a blur.

Rafael said something and took the phone from her limp fingers. She heard Molly sounding breathless and excited.

Why don't I feel that way? Why am I not happy?

"I think she's in shock. I'll have her call you later, Molly. Thank you." Rafael sounded warm and sincere and almost as though he was speaking through laughter.

He was happy. She could hear it.

"Agápi mou?" He clicked off her phone and set it aside, then drew her from her chair. "There it is. We've done it."

No, they hadn't. *She* hadn't.

"You're shaking." He hugged her, still sounding as though he was chuckling over her reaction.

"Anything could still go wrong," she blurted, wedging her arms between them.

Not that she wanted anything to go wrong. No. Absolutely not. She wouldn't wish Molly to go through a miscarriage or any sort of trauma.

The magnitude was hitting her, though, of exactly what she was asking from her friend. Why would Molly agree to this?

I don't deserve it.

Rafael kept his arms around her as he studied her through hooded eyes.

She swallowed, realizing she was displaying all the wrong reactions.

"Everyone knows you're not supposed to tell people until

three months have gone past. I don't want to b—" *Become attached.* "Believe it until I know it's really going to happen."

She brushed free of his arms and moved to the rail.

"I don't want my parents to know. They *can't* know," she added, turning her head to impress that on him. "Humbolt will definitely start shoring up his position." He still had control of the bulk of the estate. Portions were designated for her mother's use for her lifetime, which was the excuse Humbolt used to muck with everything. "I wouldn't put it past him to find Molly and harass her..." Expose everything. Endanger the baby.

"Once the b-baby arrives, the whole arrangement shifts," she continued. "I'll finally be able to oust him. I can't risk him being forewarned."

"Is that the only reason you've wanted a baby?" Rafael's voice chilled with cynicism.

"No." She flung around to face him, still dizzy.

If that was all she wanted, she could have revealed Libby years ago. She had thought about doing it thousands of times, but that baby—Molly's little sister—was not a weapon. Sasha had always believed that the most loving, selfless, maternal thing she could do for Libby was to allow her to live outside the nest of deadly spiders she'd grown up in, but it was hitting her that she was about to bring a new baby into that.

What had she done?

And there was Rafael looking at her as though he didn't recognize her.

"No." Her voice was still strained, but she forced herself to pull it together. "But it *is* my money. My father intended it for me and my children. I refuse to let Humbolt keep his foot on my neck. You wouldn't, in my shoes. Would you? You'd fight as dirty as you had to."

"True." His mouth was stern as he watched her through the screen of his lashes, looking impossibly handsome when he was like this—still and severe, freshly showered and his shirt open at the throat. "But financial gain wasn't the first thing that leapt to mind when I heard we have a baby on the way."

"I guess that makes you a better person than me, doesn't it?" she said scathingly, before turning back to the rail and the view. She didn't see anything but a blur, though. She only saw that the baby wasn't fixing anything between them at all. How had she thought it could? How was she still making wrong decisions this late in the game?

No. It wasn't a wrong decision. She wanted her baby. Rafael's baby.

Oh, God. She buried her face in her hands, not sure she could handle how badly she wanted the baby Molly carried. If it failed to arrive...

"Alexandra." His hands closed over her upper arms and his voice was gentler as he spoke behind her ear. "I refuse to have a fight when we've just received such happy news. You *are* happy, aren't you? Because you've left it late to change your mind."

"I *am* happy," she insisted. She turned to face him, eyes hot with tears she was fighting not to allow to fall. "But I'm scared." She was rarely this honest with him about her feelings, but they bubbled up out of her. "I'm scared it won't work and we'll be back to square one. I'm scared—" To be a mother.

Her voice hiccuped into a painful bubble that was caught in her throat.

This time she would keep her baby. She would have to learn how to guide it through all the trials of life. What the hell did she know about loving and caring for someone? Teaching them how to be good and kind?

"What happens if I'm a terrible mother?" she asked in a choke. "What if I ruin our child?"

"Ruin? Or spoil?" He brushed a stray tendril of hair from where it tickled her cheek and tucked it behind her ear. "I'm sure we'll both be overindulgent, but even if we make mistakes, I'm not worried. Your mother is incompetent at best and you turned out beautifully."

"Ha!" she barked and fresh tears pushed against the backs of her eyes. Her chest hurt. Really hurt. She kept her arms wedged between them, resisting him and what he'd just said because he was *wrong*.

"So you were an unruly party girl for a few years." He laced his fingers behind her lower back. "That's what makes you interesting."

Most of her stories on that front were exaggerated or appropriated from her friends' exploits. It had always served her to be seen as wild. It drove her parents up a wall and threw them off the scent of what she'd really been up to at sixteen.

"Alexandra." His hand burrowed under her hair and cupped the side of her neck. "Every parent has moments of self-doubt. I'm sure we'll have many, but we're a good team. We've proven that."

A good team. Her heart panged. Was that all she was to him? Someone who wore the same jersey?

"We'll get through whatever we face so long as we do what we've always done—be honest with each other."

She swallowed back another scoffing, *Ha!* Her eyes refused to lift higher than the buttons on his shirt, fearing he would see how much she was hiding.

"You are always honest with me, aren't you?" he pressed.

Her pulse seemed to beat harder against the palm that still rested against her throat.

"Yes." Her voice rasped over what felt like a lie. She *was* honest with him.

But not transparent.

"Let's not borrow trouble, then. If something happens, we'll deal with it together." He drew her into his embrace once more, urging her to melt against him. His mouth pressed to her temple and his voice held a note of awe. "Let's take a moment to celebrate our first baby being on the way."

His first.

Her whole body checked, but she made herself override her stiffness and hugged him while hiding her face in the hard plane of his chest.

They were back in Athens when Rafael realized he had expected the baby news would restore their marriage to the way things had been before they had embarked on trying to start a family.

It wasn't like him to delude himself. He was an unapologetic realist, but it struck him rather hard when he realized the distance between him and his wife was growing, not shrinking.

She still had conflicted feelings around her own fertility, he supposed.

They'd had to take mandatory counseling sessions before Dr. Narula was willing to allow Molly to surrogate so he had as good an understanding as a man could have of how Alexandra might be struggling with a sense of failure or inadequacy, especially now that they were relying on someone else to carry their baby.

He had mixed feelings about the process himself. As Alexandra had said the first time they'd considered "other options," using a surrogate felt as though they were allowing a stranger to infiltrate their marriage.

Not that he had any quarrel with Molly. He found her to be pleasant and eager in the way of an A-student who wished to earn top marks for baby-building. She might be doing this for financial gain, but she wasn't greedy about it.

On the contrary, she had brought a sensible figure to the table based on the going rates in the U.S. and other countries that allowed compensation for this particular service. She had asked him to cover expenses like health care, maternity clothes, and putting her career on hold, but it was all very reasonable.

She'd been appalled when Rafael added a zero to the end of her opening ask, then tried to talk him down, which had been amusing. He related to her, though. She wasn't an orphan, but she came from humble, middle-class roots and brought those practical sensibilities with her along with a streak of ambition. Hers wasn't nearly as cutthroat as his own, but he respected her for having one.

She had also brought up a number of considerations he hadn't thought of himself, proving she took this task very seriously.

From the beginning, she had been accommodating and discreet, happily signing a nondisclosure agreement while she went through the early tests. Once she was determined to be a healthy and suitable candidate, and they decided to proceed, they had sat down to negotiate the actual surrogacy agreement. Molly had raised intelligent questions around what would happen if they were unable to take custody or some other misfortune befell any of them. She had been all business and very flexible on every point except two.

"With regards to the nondisclosure agreement, I would like to include my mother in this process moving forward. She's a midwife and very well versed in patient confidentiality. You won't have any concerns around that side of it and she will be an enormous emotional support and resource for me."

"We can agree to that," Alexandra had said promptly, despite the fact that she was the one who always insisted on profound secrecy.

Rafael found it odd that she was so willing to trust someone she'd never met, given she was such an alarmist where her parents were concerned. He understood her concerns around them, but often wondered what she thought they could do to her at this stage. She was an adult, married, living away from them. Given his growing assets, she didn't need the fortune that was supposed to come to her. He understood and respected her desire to take possession of what belonged to her, but he wasn't afraid to put her stepfather through the wash and hang him out to dry in the courts— or physically, if necessary—should Humbolt truly misbehave, yet she seemed to feel her stepfather held something over her.

There were times he wanted to prod her on that, but one of the strengths of their relationships was the boundaries they drew around their pasts. They accepted each other as they were right now, which was exactly the way he wanted it.

But given how carefully she managed what her parents knew about her life, he was surprised that she was willing to air their private business to some unknown woman in America who lived only one state over from them.

His wife and their surrogate seemed to have forged an immediate connection, however. As soon as Alexandra agreed that Molly could tell her mother, Molly smiled with relief. Her "Thank you" almost seemed to transmit more than gratitude. A silent message?

The hairs on the back of his neck stood up. What—

"I understand you'll want a thorough background check on me and my mother." Molly addressed that to Rafael. "I will consent to that and I'm confident my mother will, but within that agreement, I want your promise that you will not delve into my sister's birth history. She knows she's adopted, but it's for her to pursue the identity of her birth parents if or when that becomes something she wants. It's not your place to reveal that and that information has no relevance here."

Her gaze slid to Alexandra and she quickly spoke for both of them *again*.

"Rafael understands that sort of intrusion very well. It's public knowledge that he's adopted, but there have been times that's been used against him. He wouldn't do that to a helpless child." The look she sent him was both challenge and wariness, like the point of a knife under his chin, daring him to contradict her.

He didn't know which shocked him more, that she was putting words in his mouth or that she would doubt his ethics on this front. That *hurt*, which wasn't something that happened often. He and Alexandra had a perfect relationship—one that was affectionate enough to let down his guard with her more than he did with anyone else, but superficial enough that he was rarely stung more deeply than ego level when they argued.

"It's true," he said briskly, steeling himself against those harsh memories of being kicked to the ground and called every sort of name. Bastard. Imposter. *Garbage.* "I don't see any reason to find her birth parents since they're firmly out of her life and won't impact ours. I agree to leave her out of the screening."

Was it his imagination or did Alexandra exhale when he agreed to that?

He glanced at her, but she was adjusting herself in her seat and flicking her hair behind her shoulder, smiling blandly at Molly.

"Let's move on to how we'll keep your pregnancy under wraps once it becomes obvious," Alexandra said.

"I can take a medical leave from work. I've looked into it and they don't need to know what it's for," Molly said. "As much as I would love my mother to attend the birth, that would require my going back to America. I don't think that's ideal for the level of privacy you're seeking. As long as I'm given consistent care, I'm open to delivering wherever it suits you best. Athens, perhaps?"

"She could stay at the island villa once she's showing." Alexandra glanced at him. "It's private, but only a short helicopter flight to Athens when she goes into labor."

"Would you stay there with me?" Molly brightened as she looked to Alexandra.

"Why?" Rafael interjected flatly, instantly feeling threatened for no reason that he could fathom.

"To bond with the baby." Molly blinked in surprise, as though that should be obvious.

"Oh." He looked at his wife.

Alexandra did that thing where she dropped her lashes and painted a bored expression across her face, completely masking her thoughts.

"Let's see how things go," she murmured, not committing.

The legal side of things wrapped up very neatly after that. Before he knew it, they were getting the call on the terrace in Rio. The pregnancy was confirmed. Their baby was only the size of a kidney bean, but was already taking up all his thoughts, filling him with more anticipation than he had expected to feel.

He would swear he wasn't a sentimental man, but there was something very elating in knowing he had a baby on the way, one who was a mix of him and Alexandra. A link that could never be undone.

Why? He was enlightened enough to know that masculinity was a construct, not something that was proven by procreation. He had taken on his adoptive father's name and business, making them his own. There was no reason to feel he couldn't have done the same with a baby who did not share his bloodline.

Others placed importance on those things, however, which definitely played a part in his sense of satisfaction. A dynasty was not built on one man clawing his way to the top. An heir represented continuity. For that reason, he wanted to tell the world that he did, indeed, have a baby on the way. It was a final checkmate in the external chess game he'd been playing since he'd taken over his father's business.

His mother hadn't had the capacity to fend off the sharks that had come circling back then, the ones who'd been frenzied by the scent of blood in the water. Those predators hadn't taken him seriously and even the employees had smirked at a teenager ordering fully grown men back to work. The only authority he'd had at the time was his status as "heir" and many had tried to dismiss it as an illegitimate title.

So yes, having a baby with his DNA mattered, but that wasn't the source of this simmering satisfaction. This was a sensation of being pulled toward something bright and solid. It was an indelible connection to his wife.

That was it. That was the reason for his sense of triumph. It wasn't the achievement of making a baby. It was the unbreakable bond their baby represented.

Why was it so important, he wondered with a twinge of unease? It smacked of a sop against uncertainty, something he refused to let himself feel.

But his wife seemed so damned elusive and unpredictable these days! He couldn't help feeling he needed all the hooks and grapples he could get to hold on to her. The baby was due around Christmas, but he wanted to hurry the time away. He wanted to begin planning for this addition to their family, accumulating more evidence of their baby's impending arrival.

Instead of sharing his enthusiasm, however, Alexandra grew tetchy and obstructive. She constantly reminded him that, "Anything could happen."

At the same time, she became scrupulous about protecting Molly's interests, chasing down every promised chunk of money to ensure it was sent on time. Molly's compensation was tiered so that she received funds every week of pregnancy, but those payments were automatic.

"Did she say there was a problem with the transfer?" Rafael asked Alexandra.

"No, but I want to be sure she's being looked after. She has morning sickness. I think we should give her a bonus for putting up with that."

"That's covered under the contract. If she's too unwell to work, she can go on leave early and we'll replace her salary." Once she stopped working, she would move into the island villa, where they would provide everything she needed until the baby arrived. On delivery, Molly would receive her final payment and go back to her career.

"For God's sake, Rafael. Quit being such a hard-ass," Alexandra snapped. "You have no idea what she's going through."

"No," he agreed. "I don't. Ask her to include me in your text chain."

"It's girl stuff," she argued. "She doesn't want to share those sorts of details with you."

"Nevertheless." Rafael kept a firm grip on his patience. "I want updates. I can't help wondering if she's manipulating you—"

"Do *not*." She clasped her phone to her chest as though he were physically trying to take it from her. "I know what being manipulated feels like. That is *not* what she's doing. She mentioned it was a rough week and Dr. Narula said her checkup was fine, that she can keep working if she wants to, but *I* want to be sure we're doing everything we can to make this as easy as possible for her."

In moments like this, he was both heartened and suspicious.

"Are you worried about the baby or Molly?"

A stunned pause, then, "*Both*. Obviously."

She rose to stalk away.

"Alexandra." He took a long step to catch her wrist, keeping her beside him. "This is guilt, then?"

For one second, there was such a look of naked culpability on her face, his heart bounced in reaction. Then she pulled free.

"This isn't like asking the maid to pick up the dry cleaning. We're not putting her out for five minutes. Her entire life will be going on hold."

"Yes, but she understood that was the nature of the assignment. Didn't she? Ask her to call us when she has a moment." He nodded at her phone. "I'd like to speak with her."

"Why?" Her hand tightened on her phone again and her jaw set. He could see all sorts of angry thoughts brewing behind her expression.

"Because I want to know how she's feeling." Mentally and physically.

"*Fine,*" she said through her teeth.

What the hell?

That was the moment he realized that he had thought they would return to the more relaxed, comfortable dynamic of their early marriage. Instead, there seemed to be yet another layer of tension.

Perhaps Alexandra was simply worried about the baby. If Molly wasn't feeling well, that would trigger her concern for the baby. That made sense, he supposed.

Molly called the next day to reassure them that everything was going well, mentioning the morning sickness was an inconvenience, not severe. She urged them not to worry.

They saw her in person a few weeks later, when they flew to London for her twelve-week scan. She seemed to be her bright, happy self, smiling in greeting when they entered the clinic to find her already there.

The women embraced like long-lost friends, which didn't really surprise Rafael. They texted often and seemed to be growing closer by the day. It did strike Rafael as strange, though. Alexandra was usually aloof with everyone, even women she'd known since her school days.

"Ugh, Sash. Don't hug me so hard," Molly protested with pained humor. "I drank half the Thames to get ready for this."

"Oh. Sorry." Alexandra chuckled.

Molly left with a nurse a moment later to change into a gown.

"Did she call you Sash?" Rafael asked.

"Hmm? Oh. Yes. Short for Sasha." Alexandra began rummaging in her purse. "She told me she had a child-hood friend who had my name and went by Sasha. It's cute, right? I said she could call me that." She ran some balm across her lips and dropped the tube back into her purse, not meeting his eyes.

"Sasha is already short," he pointed out, puzzled by ex-actly how close they seemed to have become. Exactly how often did they talk?

"Mr. and Mrs. Zamos?" A nurse escorted them down a short hallway into a darkened room. Molly was on a table. A sheet was draped across her upper thighs and tucked into the waistband of, presumably, her underwear. Her hospi-tal gown was bunched up to her rib cage, exposing a belly that was still very flat.

The doctor had said this was an external scan and would only proceed to internal if that was deemed necessary, but Rafael still hesitated, feeling as though he was walking into something too personal.

Alexandra hurried toward the bed, though, and clasped Molly's hand. "Okay?"

"Mmm-hmm," Molly said. "Excited."

Rafael stood behind Alexandra and clasped her upper arms as they all looked at the screen.

The technician started with gray scale, two-dimensional imaging, pointing out the baby's heartbeat.

Both women caught their breath. Rafael let out a surreptitious breath of relief.

But as the tech took various measurements, changing the view, reality began to sink in. That was their *child*. Not just his progeny, not just an extension of Alexandra, but it would look like her and show pieces of her remarkable personality. A high-pitched voice would ask impossible questions and small legs would jump off too-high ledges and someday get behind the wheel of a car.

His heart began to thud harder. Energy gathered in him, a force that wanted to close his hands protectively around that small form and guard that life with his own.

The technician switched to a three-dimensional image. A fully formed fetus appeared on the high-def screen in shades of peach-yellow. The baby crooked one knee to block identifying its sex, then, much like a tourist in a hammock, yawned and stretched.

They all chuckled. Except Alexandra. She released a choked noise and her shoulders convulsed in his grip. She suddenly ripped herself away from him and headed out the door.

"Sasha!" Molly cried.

"Alexandra!" he said at the same time and hurried after her.

She was already pushing into the powder room across

the hall and locked him out as he arrived at the door. He bit back a curse.

Molly came out of the exam room a moment later, still wearing the hospital gown.

"Seriously?" she asked as she realized the door was locked. She rapped on it. "Sasha. Don't make me pee on the floor."

The lock clicked and Molly slipped inside, but Alexandra didn't come out. The lock clicked again.

CHAPTER SEVEN

"WHAT THE HELL was that about?" Rafael asked when they entered the hotel suite they were using here in London.

"I had a wobble," Sasha said, playing off her breakdown as though it was nothing.

"A *wobble*?"

"I got emotional. You're constantly worrying that I don't really want this baby. Surely it makes you happy that I—" Her throat closed.

Don't cry. Not again.

She had already soaked Molly's shoulder.

Her phone pinged. It was the clinic sending photos of the scans along with a confirmation that the pregnancy appeared to be progressing without issue.

She couldn't look at that image again. It flashed her back to her own scan twelve years ago. The intense longing that followed was too painful to bear.

I want my baby.

That's what she'd been thinking as she saw the tiny image that Molly carried. She wanted that baby and she wanted her first one. She wanted her bab*ies*.

And she felt set apart from both of them. Some of that was her own doing. She was deliberately keeping herself from Libby's life. She told herself it was for the girl's well-being, but it was also because she wasn't ready to untangle her feelings over giving birth and relinquishing Libby to adoption. She sure as heck wasn't ready to articulate any of that to Rafael.

"Maybe you should check in with the counselor once we're home," Rafael suggested.

"I'm sure she'll say this is normal," she dismissed.

He snorted.

"Normal for people in our situation." Was it, though? She felt as though she was walking farther and farther onto ice that was beginning to crack. The shards would shred her on the way through before frigid waters closed over her, suffocating her completely.

She stood at the window looking out, not wanting Rafael to see how fragile she was. How close to her breaking point.

"Now that the scan had confirmed everything is fine, Molly said she'll put in her request for leave. She's not showing yet so she thinks she'll stick it out another four to six weeks."

"Is that what you talked about when you were locked in the toilet with her for thirty minutes?"

"Oh, my God, Rafael! Do you really want to know what I said?" She flung around to face him, feeling persecuted. "I told her that as grateful as I am, I resent her, too, because this has come so easily to her. I'm the one who should be carrying our baby." She stabbed at her own chest.

He sucked in a breath and his head went back.

Molly hadn't been shocked by her words, probably because the counselor had warned them both that Sasha might feel this way. Sasha had apologized even as she said it and Molly hadn't taken any of it to heart. They had hugged it out while Sasha spilled out all her worries about becoming a mother. Her fear of being a bad one.

"When we married, you said you would need an heir. I'm trying to give you one." Jagged sensation tore up her voice. "I can't help that this has been hard for me."

"I know it has." His expression flexed with torture. He lifted his hand to rub the anguish off his face. "If I had known—"

"Don't," she warned coldly. "Don't say you wouldn't have come this far because I want that baby. But I don't know what you want from *me*."

"I want my wife back," he said with blistering frustration. "This…" He waved at her from eyebrows to open-toed pumps. "I don't know who this is. You're becoming a stranger."

She choked on a humorless laugh, turning her face to the window again because this person was closer to the real her than the woman he'd been living with for the last three years. Sasha was broken and messy and tired of making the best of the choices she'd made, but she didn't know how to make new ones. Not without losing the pieces of this life that she valued. Like him.

She couldn't tell him that, though, could she? Not if he was already frustrated that she wasn't the superficial socialite he'd married. Did he really want her to be that and only that?

Despair thickened her tone as she said wearily, "I don't know you, either, Rafael."

"How is that possible? I'm exactly the man I was when we married. Only richer," he said pithily.

"Exactly. I don't know anything more today than I did three years ago." She rounded on him again. "I know your parents' names and where the marina was located. I know you once got arrested for breaking into it, but what happened after that? Who bailed you out? Why do you have a scar under your chin that is so thin and straight that it looks like it came from a knife? Hmm?"

His expression shuttered, exactly the way it always did if she brought up something he preferred to pass off as "nothing worth talking about."

"I know the deal with Gio will put you into the Nine Zeroes club, but all you talk about is how quickly you might double it. Why isn't one billion enough? Why does it have to be two? You say you want this baby, but why? So you can task them with all this work that makes you so short-tempered?"

"I'm not short-tempered," he bit out.

"We promised never to lie to each other," she shot back.

"Fine. I'm not short-tempered about work. It's this." He pointed at her. "You fell apart in the doctor's office, but won't tell me why. Is that really all you talked about? You needed thirty minutes to tell Molly you have complicated feelings about her carrying our baby? Why the hell are you so reluctant to tell *me*?" The last came out like the dying breath of a dragon.

"Because you don't want to hear it! You sure as hell don't want to give me the same courtesy. Did you hear yourself just now? I asked you a half dozen questions and you turned it around on me, not answering a single one of them."

"My mother bailed me out," he muttered as though it was obvious. "And you want money as much as I do." He turned away to pour a drink at the sideboard.

"No. I want *my* money. I don't want to let someone take what belongs to me. That's different from wanting to collect it and hoard it and use it to take over the world. Why are you so determined to do that?"

He stood very still. She could only see his profile, but she saw his cheek tick. Otherwise, he was like a statue. He blinked and finished pouring.

"I'm not as mysterious as you want to believe. I've told you there were criminal elements that threatened my father's business. That left me with a distaste for being at anyone's mercy. Money is power and that's why I like having an abundance of it." He turned to face her as he sipped. "None of that means I don't want to hear about the things that worry you. I can't fix it if you don't tell me what's broken."

"*We're* broken. How can you not see that?" she cried.

"We're going through a rough patch," he dismissed as he lifted the drink to his lips. "A lot is changing very quickly. We'll adapt and be fine."

Profound disappointment rang through her. How could she show him where and how she was broken if he wasn't willing to do the same?

"I will always be here for you, Alexandra. You can trust me. I hope you believe that."

She didn't. That was the hard truth of the matter. Every time she thought about revealing her secrets and her heart, she remembered how he had praised her for her self-sufficiency the day they married. She was the isolated yin to his autonomous yang.

That was the reason she was afraid to breathe. She felt as though she stood alone on a pile of crumbling rocks that would disappear at any moment and didn't trust him to catch her.

He swallowed his drink in two gulps. "I'll get some work done before we go out tonight."

She couldn't think of anything she wanted to do less than attend a premiere, then rub elbows with famous stars, politicians, and dry-necked aristocrats.

"I'll have a nap," she claimed, doubting she'd get a single wink.

For the first time, he left without kissing her or even looking back.

For the next three weeks, they went through the motions of their marriage, but things remained off.

It was as much Rafael's fault as Alexandra's. She had asked him for basic facts about himself and he hadn't wanted to share them.

Why did he need a billion dollars? Twice? So he would always have a bed and a solid roof and he wouldn't have to hide like a rodent behind a dumpster. So he could prove that he was worthy of his wife.

In many ways, he was more similar than different from the criminals who had extorted from his father. In order to best them, he'd had to meet them at their level. He had paid protection fees and bribes and even turned to blackmail a time or two. He had run cons and double-crossed devils. He had felt the blade of a knife score the skin of his throat and had taken that knife then used it to send his opponent running, trailing red.

That the man had subsequently died was as much the fault of the illegal doctor who had treated him as the wound Rafael had inflicted. Rafael could call it self-defense, but it didn't erase the literal blood on his hands.

Eventually, he'd been deemed impossible to kill or cow. Since then, he had been able to stay this side of the law, but that only encouraged challenges from legitimate players—

who all pretended their own fortunes hadn't been built on long-ago piracy and privateering and other unsavory acts.

The rise from middle-class roots to millionaire was the story he preferred to tell. No one, least of all his wife, needed to know he came from the gutter. It was too humiliating to revisit. Irrelevant. He much preferred her to see him as he was now—rich and successful. Powerful. Untouchable.

He preferred to blame their surrogate for the growing distance in their relationship, rather than this wall he kept so stubbornly around himself.

At least Molly didn't seem to intrude on their sex life. He and Alexandra made love with frequent and devastating passion, which was the reason it didn't bother him that Molly hadn't yet left her employment. Alexandra was talking about joining her on the island when she moved to their villa and that thought caused an itch of possessiveness inside his chest.

They were in Rome, getting ready for a gala, when Alexandra frowned at her phone "Hmph."

"What's wrong?"

"I'm not sure. Molly says, 'Everything is fine, but I've hit a snag with putting in my notice. Call when you have a minute so I can explain.'" Alexandra's attention skimmed past him to where her team of stylists were arriving, wheeling in a rack of gowns and carrying their cases of implements into the spare bedroom of their hotel suite. Her shoulders fell. "I'll call her tomorrow. After we get tonight out of the way."

Tonight's gala was an important one. Ostensibly, it was an art auction to raise funds for orphaned children, something Rafael was more than happy to support, but the attendees were tycoons from across Europe. He and

Alexandra had been given a seat at Table One. It was the equivalent of being given the secret handshake and a decoder ring. Rafael was taking his place as One Of Them.

Whether Gio Casella would be at that table remained to be seen. Rafael's almost inked deal with him was definitely the reason Rafael was being seated there. The rumor of their budding partnership was giving the impression Rafael was a direct vector to the Casella Corporation, exactly as Rafael had hoped. Accepting the royal treatment for that was a tiny bit premature, but only by a few days. He and Gio were scheduled to meet in Athens for a photo op next week.

Perhaps he *had* been testy about work, Rafael acknowledged with an inward sigh. This partnership and the benefits it would bring were looming large in his mind, but maybe he should let that be enough for a while.

He mentally scoffed at himself. Him? Take his foot off the accelerator? That wasn't in his nature. But he definitely needed to give more attention to his marriage, especially with the baby coming.

He left the suite for a few hours. He had meetings, but he picked up a peace offering for Alexandra and returned to dress in his tuxedo.

Her stylist had sent him a snapshot of the strapless corset gown she'd chosen, so he knew the collar of five strings of diamonds would suit it. A radiant-cut pink diamond would sit in the hollow of her throat and match the watermelon pink of the silk she wore.

That should have meant he was prepared when she emerged from the bedroom, but even though he regularly saw her in glamorous regalia, she still had the power to squeeze the breath from his lungs. She wore long pink gloves and upswept hair and glossy pink lips.

In contrast, her blue eyes seemed to shimmer like a mountain lake that beckoned in the distance but couldn't be reached. Not easily.

"You look beautiful. Any further adornment is superfluous," he said with the throwaway charm he had cultivated as carefully as the rest of his image. "But this is an important night for us. I wanted to mark the occasion."

A shadow came into her eyes. Skepticism? Disappointment?

A sting of adrenaline shot through his limbs. "You don't like it?"

"It's a lovely addition to my collection. Thank you." She turned her back, inviting him to put it on her.

His fingers were unnaturally clumsy. Those words "addition to my collection" caused his pulse to pound in his ears. For some reason, he recollected her long-ago boast that she had "*put aside a nest egg like a dragon.*" His mind raced, trying to remember the last time he'd visited their safe-deposit box. She was the one who rotated her jewelry in and out of it, depending on the events that were coming up in their calendar.

As much from habit as desire, he pressed a kiss to her nape once the necklace was secured.

She shivered, which was heartening, but then she touched the necklace and swallowed as though she found it restrictive.

Are we all right?

He didn't ask the question because he didn't want the answer, which was pure cowardice.

"This will only work if we're honest with each other."

Those words had been his. They were as true today as they'd been three years ago.

He wasn't being *dis*honest, though. He genuinely believed they would get through this. Once the baby was here—

Damn, but this baby was carrying a lot on its very tiny shoulders.

The driver buzzed to signal their car was waiting.

Alexandra smoothed her expression into the haughty one that the paparazzi loved to capture, but she was uncharacteristically quiet at the party. Normally, she would extend herself, entertaining their table with anecdotes and cheeky wit, winning everyone over.

Tonight, she barely seemed to be in the room. When he held her on the dancefloor, she was stiff with tension, her face a cool mask he could hardly read.

"Are you not feeling well? You've been quiet."

"I can't stop thinking about Molly. She should have given notice right after the twelve-week scan. It's coming up to fifteen. I know Gio's been traveling and she wants to do it in person, but she's putting on weight. Someone is bound to guess—"

"Can we have one conversation where we don't talk about her?" he asked curtly.

She drew her head back in shock.

"She's an adult who knows her assignment," he continued stiffly. "If she's worried about discovery, she should put in a request for a medical leave and *leave*."

"She's a conscientious person—"

"Yes, I know that. That's why there's no reason for you to worry about her. She'll figure it out."

"You really don't care about her at all." Her arms dropped away from him.

"I care about her the exact amount that is appropriate for

her place in our life. *You* care about her too much. I don't understand why."

She took that like a slap. She was stunned, cheeks flushing with angry heat.

Rafael was aware of people noting that they had stopped dancing. It wasn't the type of stir he liked to create.

With his heart pinballing in his chest, he drew her off the dance floor and into a quiet corner of the room.

"What is going on?" he demanded.

Her mouth parted, closed. She shook her head helplessly, then searched his eyes.

"Are you happy, Rafael?"

"Of course," he stated promptly. "We're achieving everything we set out to achieve." He nodded toward the room at large, where he'd been welcomed warmly all evening. "Once the deal is signed with Gio, my position will be secure." He would always have room for growth, but there would be less chance of a serious backslide into losing everything. "My heir is on the way and you'll soon have the means to pry your stepfather off your fortune. This is a very good moment for us."

"But what about *us*? Babies put more pressure on a marriage, not less. We're in trouble, Rafael."

"It's nothing we can't fix." She was taking sandpaper to his organs. He looked around, but people had lost interest in them. He still felt the heat of a spotlight.

"How?" she asked with misery. "This isn't about the baby. It's about *us*. Sometimes I think that if you loved me, I could trust you enough to…" Her desolate gaze cast about the room, looking for something that had him tensing as though bracing for a blow.

This was edging into places he had closed off a long

time ago, places that she occupied to some extent, but he was careful about how far inside him she infiltrated. Otherwise, he would be too exposed. Too vulnerable.

"Love is a liability." It was power. If you gave it to someone, they held that power over you. Or they could be used against you. Your own feelings could be. "We agreed on a partnership that benefits both of us," he reminded her.

She looked at him with profound disappointment. "Yes, well, you said I've changed and I have. I've fallen in love with—"

The gravel in his stomach turned to curdled milk. His ears filled with water.

"—you."

His relief was so intense, he laughed. "I thought you were going to say Molly."

"What?" She snapped her head back. "No! You. Although God knows why." Her eyes gleamed with angry tears. "I love *you*, Rafael. And you don't love me back. Do you?"

His next breath came in like powdered glass. In some ways, it glinted like magic dust, filling him with an unfamiliar type of joy, but another part put the brakes on. Hard.

Was she even telling the truth? There had been a time when he wouldn't doubt her word, when he would believe anything she told him because they were always honest with each other. They might not have married for love, but they had trust.

Or did they? He had begun to suspect there was much more he ought to know, but she was a closed book.

"Love wasn't something we expected to happen, was it?" It was a grasp of the wheel to steer them from a dangerous cliff, but he overcompensated, sounding cool and impatient when he ought to be kinder.

"You don't," she confirmed, holding his stare with betrayal clouding her eyes.

Before he could backtrack, she stalked to their table where she gathered her wrap and clutch, claimed a headache and said good-night to their tablemates.

The silence as they climbed into the car was thick enough to slice with a knife.

Rafael should have left it that way. Instead, he instructed their driver to put in his earbuds so he and Alexandra could have some privacy. He should have waited until they were back in their hotel suite. He would tell himself that again and again over the next months.

I should have waited.

But he didn't.

"I'm entitled to be surprised," he said as the car pulled into traffic "When *you* proposed to *me*—" He deliberately reminded her of that. "You told me this wouldn't happen. Our marriage is a practical one."

"And once we have what we wanted, do we stay married?"

"Don't throw out ultimatums you're not prepared to back up," he commanded.

"I'm not. Everything is in place for a clean split." She was talking about their prenuptial agreements, which had been very meticulously crafted for such an eventuality.

"We're not divorcing," he said through his teeth. "We have a baby on the way."

"I *know* that!" she cried loud enough to catch the driver's attention.

That was what Rafael would live to regret forever, that

he had prodded her into that burst of emotion. It distracted the driver long enough to touch the brakes in the middle of racing through an intersection.

If he hadn't done that, the car that was jumping the light, accelerating, would have missed their rear bumper by a hairbreadth as they zoomed beneath an amber turning red.

Instead, Alexandra's expression flashed to horror in a blinding light. There was a screech of metal and an impact that rotated the car, throwing Rafael toward her.

CHAPTER EIGHT

RAFAEL WAS BEGINNING to appreciate Alexandra's hatred toward her parents. He'd always seen her mother's superficial nature and timid deference to her husband as pitiful. Humbolt was a self-important bully who occasionally needed a threat of legal action to back off, but he was a coward at heart so he didn't deserve to be feared.

Then Rafael overheard them trying to transfer his unconscious wife to New York and nearly came out of his skin.

They must have heard about the crash on the news and leaped on the first plane to Rome, but their concern was very much for themselves, not Alexandra.

"A move like that would be dangerous." That Italian-accented voice sounded like one of their doctors. "We haven't detected any bleeding on the brain, but we're presuming concussion and treating her accordingly."

"But why isn't she waking up? We can get better treatment in America," Winnie Humbolt claimed.

Better than a world-class private hospital in Rome? Rafael's driver had been conscious enough to identify them to the medics, ensuring they were given top-level care from the moment they arrived. The driver was also receiving treatment here and thankfully would make a full recovery.

Rafael wouldn't take a full breath until he heard the same thing about his wife, though.

"We're keeping her sedated as a precaution," the doctor said in a placating tone.

"Tell your chief of staff to make the arrangements." Anson Humbolt used the brisk tone of a man who was used to stepping on people to get what he wanted.

"Doctor," Rafael rasped in the strongest voice he could muster. It made his entire body throb.

A man in a white coat pushed through the cracked door, revealing Winnie and Anson Humbolt hovering in the hall, looking wrinkled and weary from travel.

"If you allow them to take my wife anywhere, you are the second person I will kill on the way to getting her back." Humbolt would be the first.

It was a laughable threat, given he was still swimming in anesthetic from the surgery he'd had last night, to pin his broken leg. He could only see out of one eye and the twenty stitches on his arm gave him only one good one for swinging a punch, but he meant every word.

"Rest, signore," the doctor urged him. "Your wife is stable and her vitals are strong. She isn't going anywhere until she wakes and we can assess her condition."

Aside from hitting her head on the window and bruises from her seat belt, she had escaped serious injury, but he wished they would wean her off the sedation so he could see that for himself. The physical pain in his body was nothing compared to the urgency to know she was all right.

It took another day. The doctor told him in the morning that they would ease up her medication, but it would take until later in the afternoon for her to come to.

Rafael was dozing off the semisolid meal they'd fed him,

trying to ignore the acute pain he was in, but he was keeping his own dosage of painkillers light, wanting to be sharp enough to monitor everything that happened across the hall.

When he heard Winnie cry, "Doctor! She's awake," he urgently thumbed the call button until his nurse hurried in to see him.

"Get me to her," he ordered.

A burly orderly appeared, but moving off his bed into a wheelchair was an ordeal that almost had Rafael fainting from the pain. His need to see Alexandra was all-encompassing, though. He gritted his teeth and waved an impatient hand.

He was pushed into her room in time to hear her say, "No. I don't know who these people are."

"What about me?" he demanded.

The figures gathered around the bed parted, allowing him to see the pale, delicate face of his wife. Her expression widened in alarm at his bruised, beat-up, unshaven face.

Was that fear that flashed behind her eyes? He reached out to take her hand.

"You know who I am. Don't you?" How could she not? They were two sides of the same rare coin.

Everything is in place for a clean split.

No. Absolutely not. It wasn't possible. Besides, she loved him. She'd said so.

But she shook her head, which had him feeling as though his insides were wedged open.

"I'm your husband. Rafael." Was he missing something in his own drug-addled state? Surely, she couldn't have forgotten him. *Them.*

She only stared at him blankly.

Through his shock, he realized her parents were pressuring her to come home with them.

"No." It didn't matter whether Alexandra knew him or them or herself. *He* knew she would never forgive him if he let them take custody of her. He would never forgive himself. "Alexandra is my wife. She comes home with me."

What have I done? Sasha wondered as they left the hospital for their private jet a few days later.

Right up until she was climbing into the car, her parents had kept up their pressure for her to go back to America with them. It had only fueled her ruse that she didn't recognize them. She knew it was childish. Unethical. Cruel, even, especially to Rafael.

But she was angry with him, too. All she could think about what how truly degrading it had felt when he had laughed—*laughed*—at her declaring her love for him. Why did she have to love him at all, especially this hard? *Why?*

"Why" didn't matter. She wasn't going to let him hold it over her. If she didn't remember saying it, it hadn't happened. Not for her.

Letting go of her memory, of her history, was enormously freeing. It allowed her to put down the burden of being Alexandra and say what was really on her mind. When her mother had noticed her broken nails and suggested a manicure, Sasha had turned up her nose.

"I don't like false nails." She didn't like a lot of things, especially criticism from her mother.

"That's not a flattering style," Winnie said when Sasha gathered her hair into a half topknot.

"It's comfortable," she said blandly, then told the nurse

she was done with visitors for the day, forcing them to be shooed out.

Without the guilt of her past as a pressure point, Humbolt was toothless, too.

"You're hurting your mother's feelings by refusing to come home with us," he said the next day, when her mother stepped out of the room to fetch coffee.

"Oh? Winnie said she wants me to stay with you because she's afraid Rafael will evict you if I don't remember you, and that you have nowhere else to go. Is that true, Anson?" she asked with baffled curiosity. "Do you not have money of your own?" She knew he didn't.

She took him aback using his first name. He stood taller and erased her words with a wave of his hand. "No, no. She wants to look after you because she cares about you."

"So you *do* have somewhere to go. Because I understand all the properties are actually mine."

"Listen, girlie. Don't try to play hardball with me." He came closer to the bed.

She picked up the call button.

His mouth tightened. Aside from taking a rough grip on her arm or other manhandling like that, he'd never been outwardly violent, but he loved to belittle her. Hundreds of times, he had turned her insides to stone with a contemptuous glower like the one he wore now.

For once, she truly felt impervious to it.

"There are things I could bring up that you'd rather weren't made public," he warned. "Things that would send your husband running and ruin your life."

"But I would still have my fortune," she clarified, tilting her head in thought. "And since I've already forgotten the life I had, it doesn't matter if you burn it down. I'll see how it goes with my husband. If things don't work out, I'll need my house. You should start making other arrangements."

He was *not* happy with her inability to be intimidated. He tried to sic her mother on her and Winnie brought to bear some of her best guilt-saturated manipulation, but a lack of memory served Sasha there, too.

"I know I should feel obligated, but I don't."

She refused to apologize for her lack of sympathy. The only thing she was sorry for was allowing Humbolt to bully her as long as he had. When they left Winnie and Anson on the sidewalk in Rome, Sasha was confident it would be the last time she ever spoke to them.

Leaving her parents in the dust seemed to be the impetus in Rafael's decision to head back to Athens, despite being told he would need another surgery.

Sasha should have stayed in hospital herself. She was mostly uninjured, but persistent headaches ran the gamut from dull to debilitating. The doctor said she should expect that to continue for weeks, possibly months, but hoped they would dwindle over time, provided she got plenty of rest and gave herself time to heal.

Rafael was limping short distances on crutches, but should be using a wheelchair. Too much stress on his forearm could pop his stitches, but she would love to meet the person who successfully told Rafael he wasn't allowed to do something.

As they boarded the jet, Sasha debated coming clean to him about her memory but a private nurse was traveling with them along with Rafael's assistant, Tino. The flight was less than two hours so they stayed in their seats, rather than move into the stateroom where they would have had more privacy.

Some of the shades were open so Sasha kept her sunglasses on. Rafael's breath rattled out as he settled into the seat beside her.

Pity for both of them rolled through her along with a tingling longing. She yearned for the comfort of his touch. She had nearly lost him!

She didn't care as much that her own life had been endangered. Her baby would be safe with Molly no matter what happened to her. She already knew that, since her first one was. Thank *God* the baby hadn't been at risk in that crash.

But nearly losing Rafael was terrifying. It made her realize how much she really did love him, even though she was still furiously angry with him.

Love is a liability.

It sure was. That's why she was pretending she hadn't offered hers to him.

She had come so close to telling him everything that night! The affair with a married man, Libby, her real relationship with Molly—whom she did love, but not in the way he'd suggested.

He had laughed at her for saying she loved him. Her trust and willingness to share had been shattered at that point. Even if he did care about her to some extent, it was only the exact amount that was appropriate for a wife who had helped him achieve what he wanted to achieve. She couldn't stand that she had practically begged him to feel more. She must seem utterly pathetic in his eyes.

As the plane took off, she glanced to see the nurse and assistant were ensconced at the back of the cabin, and turned her head to study the mottled bruise on the side of his face.

An urge to kiss it better nearly overwhelmed her, but he turned his own head to ask, "You really can't remember anything?"

She was glad she was wearing her sunglasses because her eyes reflexively widened in alarm as she felt pinned by his hard stare. She sidestepped by focusing on the memory she genuinely had lost.

"The driver told the investigators that we were arguing." An officer had come by her room to ask what she remembered of the crash. She had told him with complete honesty that she didn't recall anything about being in the car. "He said we distracted him. Is that true? Or is he trying to get out of taking responsibility?"

"It's true." Rafael's mouth flattened into a tight line. He looked forward again, eyes closing in a slow blink. "He was startled into hitting the brake and glanced back at us. He didn't see the other car jumping the light and stopped right in front of it."

Rafael had taken the brunt of that? She felt ill.

"What were we arguing about?" She could hardly speak around the lump in her chest.

He drew in a breath to speak, then let it out, seeming reluctant to answer.

"You told me you loved me. You don't remember saying that?" He turned his head again, sending the intensity of his narrow-eyed gaze across her face like a laser that left every inch of her skin feeling scorched.

Oh, God.

She used one hand to cover the other as it curled into a fist in her lap.

"How is that an argument?" her scattered brain managed to ask. "We're married. Don't we love each other?"

It was unkind of her to use her lie as a tool to poke at him and their marriage, but she had no defenses otherwise. They would be right back to that impossible cold war except he'd have her heart in his pocket. This was the only way to take herself back from him.

"I want to say yes," he admitted heavily, causing a pulsing sting to shoot through her veins. "But we made a deal when we married that we would always be honest with each other. I want to honor that."

Wow. Nothing had changed. They had nearly been killed, but it hadn't moved the dial on his feelings for her. She felt as though the floor had dropped out of the plane and she was plummeting to the earth at a million miles an hour.

She had known all along that he didn't love her, though. For a long time, it hadn't mattered. Not until they had tried to start a family and the weight of her first baby became too much to bear. If she couldn't trust him with her heart, how could she trust him with the innocent person inside it? That's what this came down to.

"So you don't love me. And that's why we were fighting?" It was painful to force this clarity, but it hardened her resolve to keep up this game. "Why are we even married?"

"I'm very fond of you—"

"Fond," she choked. "Fond is how you feel toward a great-aunt who offers you peppermints. Why did you even bring me with you today? Why not send me home with my parents if you don't care what happens to me?"

"I *care*," he said through his teeth. "You would never forgive me if I let them take you. And you're *my wife*, Alexandra. Even if you don't remember it. I protect what's mine."

She snorted, realizing she had always been one more

asset he had collected. She wanted to cry, but only closed her eyes, claiming, "I'm tired."

It must have been the truth because the next thing she knew, they had landed in Athens. Rafael was equally groggy and sullen as they were driven to an unfamiliar villa on the outskirts of Athens. It was more modest than the places they usually stayed in, but it had a pool and a casita where the nurse went to unpack.

"There are too many stairs in our home in Attica," Rafael explained as he limped into the lounge behind her. "Also, my assistant said it was staked out by paparazzi. I bought this for my mother, not that she lived to see it. An agency manages it as a vacation rental, but it happened to be empty. You've never been here so it won't be familiar to you."

Sasha took in the open plan of the main living area with its tasteful, if generic, furnishings. An L-shaped countertop divided the kitchen from the dining area and sliding doors led out to the patio.

"When did she pass?" It was a natural question to ask under the circumstance, even though she already knew the answer.

"A few months before you and I met."

He had told her that in the early days of their marriage, but had barely mentioned his parents since then. Sasha hadn't asked a lot of questions because she hadn't wanted him to pry into her own past.

That risk was no longer a factor, though. Was it?

"Were you close with her?"

After a hesitation, he said, "I'm adopted. Have you read anything about me online?"

"No." She was dying to check in with Molly, but... "My

phone is broken. The doctor said I should stay off screens anyway, because they're likely to make my headaches worse. Is that your answer? That you weren't close to your mother because you're adopted?"

He was opening the cupboards in the bottom of the china cabinet and came up with an unopened bottle of Scotch and a heavy sigh.

"I had a closer relationship to my parents than you have with yours," he said drily. "But they adopted me at eight, almost nine." He glanced up from pouring a generous amount of Scotch into a glass. "I was about as civilized as a feral cat."

She wanted to ask if he thought alcohol was a good idea, but she had never heard him describe himself that way. "How do you mean?"

"I was skittish. Didn't want to be touched. My birth mother brought me from Romania when I was four. She was trying to find my father, who was Greek, but I have come to believe he lied to her about what kind of man he was."

"Greek?"

"Rich," he clarified pithily.

He stacked his crutches under his good arm and leaned on the cabinet, then used his injured arm to lift the glass to his lips. He took a deep gulp, as though he'd been waiting a year for that alcohol to hit his bloodstream. His breath hissed out in a mix of relief and burn.

"She wasn't trying to cash in," he continued. "Only force him to support the child he'd made. I can remember her saying, 'He can give you a better life than I can. We just have to find him.' We had nothing when we arrived and never managed to accumulate more than a few blankets and enough food to keep us alive. I don't know what kind of work she did. Something menial. She would leave me with a woman I didn't understand and snot-nosed children who weren't afraid to knock me around for whatever I had that they wanted."

She couldn't help the pang of protest that resounded in her throat.

"I learned to knock back," he assured her with a negligent shrug. He gave his glass a dispassionate swirl before taking another sip. "One morning she didn't wake up. I didn't know what to do so I walked to the day care and told her. She turned me away, told me to go home. I realize now that she was afraid she would get in trouble for taking in too many children and helping illegal immigrants. She must have made a call, though. When I got back, police were there. I was taken to a home, but I ran away. I wanted to find my mother."

Her hand lifted to cover where her heart turned over in her chest, hurting for that lost little boy.

"I was on the street for three or four weeks, I guess. There was an older girl—a prostitute and way too young for it—it's all a blur, really, but she was nice to me. Taught me how to shoplift and how to find a place to sleep. I really liked her, but I was caught stealing and sent to a group home with bars on the windows. I couldn't run away and find her to tell her what had happened to me. That's always bothered me, that I didn't say goodbye to her."

He shook off the memory and gulped again from the Scotch.

"How old were you?"

"By then? Six. I overheard people talking about sending me back to Romania. I kept telling them my father was Greek, that they had to find my father. They never did.

I have no idea if they tried, but I was put in a school for troubled boys. Between the strict teachers and my fellow students and the toughs in the group home, I got plenty of lessons on how to ignore pain." He nodded at his broken leg.

As it turned out, she was glad she hadn't known this about him. It was far too painful to hear, but she stayed silent, letting him continue.

"By the time I was adopted, I was a rough piece of work, but I had come to appreciate a dry bed and regular meals. I knew how to mind my manners to get those things. I was competitive as hell and had realized there were many ways to beat someone, so my grades were top of the class. I guess that's what my parents saw in me, a boy who was intelligent enough to take over the business and hardened enough not to collapse under the pressure the local thugs put on them."

"That's a lot to ask of anyone, let alone a boy."

And why had he never told her any of this? It was taking all her control not to ask that.

"They lost their son in a drowning accident or they would have put it on him." He shrugged. "They were adamant that I wasn't a replacement for him, but what else was I?" He topped up his Scotch. "They were close to fifty when they adopted me. My mother was the driver in that, wanting someone to look after them and the business once they retired. My father and I got along well enough, but we were very different. I was ambitious and driven. He was… tired. Grief-stricken and worn down by life. We didn't talk much unless it was about the business. He didn't take care of himself. He had high blood pressure. His heart attack wasn't a shock."

"I'm so sorry," she murmured.

"When he passed, my mother was convinced the business would be stolen from her. She didn't realize what a punk I really was. That was probably my greatest con, hiding that from her," he said with a smirk. "And you, of course."

"W-what?" She was so dumbfounded by his revelations, by the fact he was sharing so much, she set a hand on the wall to keep herself from falling over.

"Will you put this on the table for me?" He held out his refilled glass.

"Yes." She reflexively hurried forward to take it, but he didn't let it go.

"You were angry with me for a lot of things," he said gravely, staring through her sunglass lenses in a way that seemed to peer all the way into her soul. "You said that in three years, I hadn't told you anything more about myself than what you knew the day we married. You weren't wrong. I *hate* talking about my childhood." He scowled with distaste. "I've always wanted you to see me as I am now, not the way I was then, but I want you to stay in this marriage. That means you need to know me enough to trust me."

"Why is it so important I stay?" If he didn't love her, if he was only "fond" of her, what did it matter what she thought of him or whether they shared a house or a bed?

Wait, was that what he wanted? Sex? She kind of did, too, but it had become really hard to engage in physical intimacy while knowing she was investing so much more of her heart than he was.

On the other hand, if he had lost his mother so tragically, then regarded himself as a replacement for a couple's "real" child, she had to wonder if he knew how to attach himself to anyone. She hadn't, not until she had been given love in its purest form. Even then, she had resisted allowing love into her life. She was resisting it again, too conscious of how vulnerable it made her.

"Let's sit down," he said, glancing toward the sofa. "There's something else you need to know. I'm not sure how you'll react."

She nervously carried his drink to a coaster on the coffee table, suspecting what was coming as she settled into the opposite corner and tried to appear appropriately curious.

He winced as he sat. His casted leg stuck out at an angle against the table legs.

"We're expecting a baby."

It took everything in her to let her lips part in shock.

Seriously, why was she continuing this stupid charade? *I know.* That's all she had to say. *I know.*

But she didn't want to go back to where they'd been at the gala. She wanted this, where he confided in her even though it was difficult for him. Would he do that if he knew she remembered everything? No. He would expect her to be Alexandra and would return to being closed-off Rafael, leaving her wondering what was going on behind his remote expression.

"How?" she asked. "The hospital didn't tell me—"

"We're using a surrogate. Molly."

She blew out a breath and covered her face with her hands, dislodging her sunglasses as she leaned her elbows onto her knees. She was mostly trying to hide the fact that this news wasn't as big a shock to her as he thought it was, but she was worried about Molly and had to press back on her instinct to ask about her.

"We were having trouble conceiving," he continued.

No, *they* weren't. His sperm had no trouble seducing

her eggs into becoming embryos. She was the one who couldn't hang on to them.

"Molly is about sixteen weeks along by now? She heard about the crash on the news and has been reaching out, but—" he cursed "—she's engaged to her boss."

"What?" Astonishment had her lifting her face from her hands.

It was a huge mistake. She had leaned forward on the sofa at just the right angle for the sunlight to glance off the pool, sifting between the furniture legs in the dining room and straight into her eyes.

She clenched her eyes shut, but the damage was done. Stars were exploding behind her eyelids.

"I know," Rafael was grumbling. "It's completely inappropriate. She signed a binding NDA to keep the pregnancy strictly confidential. I don't think she would tell him she's carrying our baby, but maybe this explains why she hasn't given her notice yet? The whole thing is suspicious. It's made worse by the fact that Gio Casella is a business partner of mine. We were about to sign off on a partnership deal a few days ago, but he put that on hold because of our crash. Now I'm afraid to talk to her in case she tells him—"

"Rafael." She weakly fluttered her hand in his direction, using the other to shield her closed eyes. A halo of pain was forming inside her skull, pressing outward. Dread and nausea combined in her middle.

He cursed and caught her hand. "Migraine?"

"Yes. I need to lie down."

"Your glasses." She heard one of his crutches tumble to the floor and winced at the noise. The cushion dipped beside her, then the sunglasses pressed into her hand. "I'll text the nurse to take you to the bedroom. I'd take you myself, but—" He cursed his crutches. "She's coming with a pain pill and ice," he said a moment later.

"Thank you," she said meekly, aware they had so much more to talk about, but right now, she needed a dark room and silence.

CHAPTER NINE

RAFAEL LOST A few more days to another surgery to adjust a pin. It was relatively minor in the grand scheme of things, but it left him bedridden and dopey, which made him grumpy.

Alexandra was marginally better. She joked that she had become a vampire, afraid to leave her room during daylight hours, but it wasn't funny. She had little color in her cheeks and her lips were often white. She didn't eat much, didn't move much, and couldn't watch television or look at a screen for more than a minute or two. Any loud noise or bright light sent her straight back to bed and a cooling eye mask.

They were sleeping apart and that bothered him most of all. He didn't expect her to run away, but he wasn't convinced she wouldn't.

He loathed any type of uncertainty and kept remembering her saying, *"Everything is in place for a clean split."*

"Are you awake?" he asked in a whisper when he finished a long day of trying to catch up on work and found her lying on the sofa in the dark, wearing pajamas and her sleep mask. A dated romcom was playing on a very low volume on the television.

"Yes." She bent her knees as an invitation for him to sit on the cushion. "Who were you yelling at?"

"I wasn't yelling, was I?" He lowered into the corner of the sofa with a hiss of weary pain, trying to recollect who he'd been speaking to.

It could have been anyone. Much was on the line if he didn't put out this dumpster fire that his life had become. He wouldn't be ruined if Gio failed to sign that deal, he kept reassuring himself. He would merely be humiliated and set back. Significantly.

Alexandra would be fine. She had always managed her own portfolio, investing with him at different times, but mostly keeping her money in relatively stable assets like real estate. He was currently leveraging against some of her assets, but there were firm firewalls in place. He'd lose everything while her fortune would barely be dented. That was both reassuring, but also galling to his ego. It probably wouldn't have bothered him so much if they were in a stronger place, but everything felt very tentative right now.

He looked to where her ankles peeked from beneath the hem of her lime green pajama pants. Her bare toes were curled. Wariness? Or sexual tension?

"Did I start one of your headaches?"

"No. You weren't loud enough for me to hear what you were saying, but I could tell you were swearing."

He had a lot to swear about these days, not least of which the fact that she was suffering. "Have you had one today?" He deliberately kept his voice quiet.

"No. But, I don't want to jinx it by bragging about it."

He smiled faintly. Sometimes she sounded exactly like the woman he knew. Other times, she was a reticent stranger. He wanted to push and prod and establish exactly where they stood, but she was so fragile he had to handle her with great care.

He guided her feet into his lap.

She resisted. "What are you doing?"

"I'll rub your feet."

"You don't have to."

"I want to."

"Why?"

Because it had been a lifetime since he'd touched her.

"To help you relax," he claimed.

A strangled noise resounded in her throat.

He smiled with amused gratification and gently crushed her feet in his closed hands before focusing on the left one.

"Isn't there some sort of therapy that uses pressure points on the foot? Perhaps I can cure your headaches for good."

"I'm ready to try anything," she said with a sigh, allowing her legs to relax. "How do you feel?"

"Fine."

"I thought we don't lie to each other." Her voice wavered between facetious and challenging.

"My leg is killing me," he admitted. "I'm tired and frustrated that I tire so easily. I'm furious that Gio is dragging his feet. It puts me in a bind."

"I keep thinking I should call her." Tension returned to her foot. "The surrogate. Molly, was it?"

"And tell her that you've forgotten she's carrying our baby?" He carefully worked his thumb against the stiffness in her arch. "I'm concerned about how close she's become to Gio."

Last he'd checked, they'd been in London, but Gio was due to come to Athens this weekend. Rafael had deliberately not spoken to him, letting their teams reschedule everything as though the crash had been a minor inconvenience and there was nothing to worry about.

"What would you say to her?" he asked. "How do you feel about becoming a mother?"

She seemed to go very still. He had the strange impression that her foot went cold in his hands.

"How do you feel about becoming a father?" she asked in a strained voice.

"We both want this baby very much," he assured her.

"You're very good at avoiding direct answers."

He would bet her brow was wrinkled in consternation behind that mask.

He sighed.

"I don't like revealing what I want," he admitted. "It allows people to use it against me. It gives them the opportunity to take my toy or hold my company hostage or threaten my parents."

"Did people do that to you?"

"Yes."

"Is that why you're so…"

"What?" he prompted.

"Hard."

"I didn't think you'd noticed."

She stole her foot from his grip and nudged his thigh, tsking.

He smirked and took up the other foot.

"Is it, though?" she asked. "Why you're so closed off and difficult to read?"

"Life is poker. It's gambles and risks and bluffs, trying to win the pot. Never let anyone know what cards you hold."

"Does that make the baby a chip? Or…?" The anxiety

in her voice had his heart swinging out and snapping back into his chest with a sting.

"No," he said firmly. "I'll admit that I had always looked on children the way my parents did. I have a business that needs an heir. Why go to the trouble of building a dynasty if it will die when I do? That's why I pressured you into starting a family."

"Did you?" Her foot twitched in his grip, but he held on to it, seizing the chance to say things he hadn't been able to say before because she'd been too defensive.

"I did." He saw that now and regretted how blithe he'd been when he brought up having a baby. He'd presumed it was simple. One more thing to tick off the list. "You seemed ready, but I think you were ambivalent, maybe doing it more for me than yourself."

I've changed. I've fallen in love with you.

He'd been thrown by that confession, but he mourned losing that woman and wished he'd reacted differently when she'd said it.

"When it didn't work out right away, you were distressed," he continued. "We couldn't have known it would be like that, but things grew difficult between us."

"In what way?" she asked in a husk of a voice, as though she wasn't sure she wanted the answer.

"You were angry with your body. I was frustrated that I couldn't give you what you want. I like giving you everything you ask for. It pleases me to spoil you. That I can."

"BDE," she said under her breath.

He froze. "You've accused me of that many times. Are you getting your memory back?"

"What? No." A small pulse seemed to cause her foot to

tic in his hands. "But I know what Big Dick Energy is and you definitely have it."

"Hmph." He went back to massaging her foot, wondering if he wanted her to get her memory back when this felt like a second chance for them. Rather than a wall between them, they had a blank slate that at least didn't have the difficult passages of their history written upon it.

"Can I ask you something?" Her voice was timid enough to stall his hands again. "How do you feel about your adoption. Like, really. Deep down?"

"I think being adopted saved my life and kept me out of jail. Mostly," he added drily. "Look, I know it was hypocritical that I wanted us to make a baby. I see now how selfish that was, considering how hard it became on you, but…" He squeezed her foot, feeling as though his lungs were being compressed, pushing out all the air. He drew in a deep breath, refilling them before he admitted, "There's something about knowing our baby is a combination of both of us that pleases me. I don't have anyone, Alexandra. Just you."

He heard her sharp inhale.

"You have your parents," he acknowledged. "But you've never had a good relationship with them. From the night we met, you made me feel as though you only had me. That you needed me as much as I needed you."

"Do you?" she asked skeptically.

"Yes. When we're on our game, we're a formidable team. Having a baby with you, one who has all the best parts of us…? Or the worst," he added with a husk of dark laughter. "Either way, I want that. I want our baby very much."

She was quiet, teeth worrying the edge of her lip.

"And you? How do you feel?" he prompted. "About becoming a mother?"

Her foot withdrew to settle beside the other one. Her upraised knees formed a barrier between them. He watched her fists close and tuck beneath her elbows in a protective hug.

"I honestly don't know," she said with quiet anguish. "I know I should be happy. I know I will love my baby. I already do." One fist moved to the spot between her breasts and she used the heel of her palm to rub her sternum, as though trying to soothe a pain there. "I can imagine holding a newborn, but I can't—I can't picture being a mother."

Her bottom lip was quivering as if she was very near tears.

"Alexandra." He looped his arm around her bent legs and set his mouth against her knee. "I'm sure that will come with time. This is a strange circumstance. It's okay that it's a shock. The baby isn't due until Christmas. You'll have time to process."

"But do you really believe we can be good parents?" She carefully lifted the edge of her mask to peer at him. "Whatever team we were before… Do you honestly believe we were strong enough to sustain twenty years together? And support our child in all the ways we'll need to? What happens between you and me in all that time?"

"We relearn how to be us. And yes, I absolutely believe we will be together for the rest of our lives."

"How can you be so sure?"

"Because I don't lose the things I value."

"I'm not a thing, Rafael. Unless you realize that, I don't know that we do have a chance." She let the mask drop back into place then rolled onto her side, knees still bent and feet jammed against the sofa back. She curled her arm beneath the cushion under her ear and listened to Richard Gere climb a fire escape to rescue Julia Roberts.

With careful management, Sasha had three days of only a leaden headache, not an incapacitating one.

"That's good," Rafael said when they were eating lunch in the dimmed light of the shuttered dining room. "You can come to the gala with me tonight."

"Why?" He might as well have suggested sending her to a work camp in Siberia. "I won't know anyone."

That was a lie, of course, but she was too deep into this bigger lie to say anything different. She couldn't seem to regret pretending her memory loss, either. He was revealing fascinating and sometimes painful things, but she was also able to be more honest about her own feelings than she had ever been before. The other night, she had told him about her ambivalence around motherhood and he'd been very sweet and nonjudgmental.

"People need to see that we're fine, Alexandra."

"We're not fine."

His gaze flashed up to hers. "We're getting along perfectly."

Perfectly was a stretch, but… "Are you going to wear those gym shorts under your tuxedo jacket?" She nodded across the table where she knew he wore gray, drawstring shorts beneath the shirt and tie that appeared on his video chats.

"My trousers will be delivered later today along with a selection of gowns. It's only an appearance," he pressed on when she wrinkled her nose. "We don't have to stay more than an hour, but it will go a long way toward convincing people that nothing has changed."

"Fine," she mumbled. She was going a little stir-crazy, so maybe a night out would do her good.

After a nap and a very subdued session with her stylist, she came out to the lounge in a bronze gown that was decorated with braided piping. It hugged her torso before the metallic silk parted dramatically to expose her left leg to the top of her thigh. Her makeup hid the fact that she'd lost a couple of pounds and still lacked color. She left her hair down, only allowing it to be straightened so it fell in a blunt line from the caramel roots to the brighter highlights of straw and gold at the ends.

Rafael had brought jewelry from the safe-deposit box, so she was already wearing the thick links of a heavy gold necklace and a wide cuff on her upper arm.

"You look beautiful," he said as she appeared in the lounge. It was lit only by one lamp. "I've always liked this on you." He hitched himself close enough to trace his fingertip along the upper edge of the cuff, lifting goose bumps from her elbow to her shoulder. Even her nipples tightened.

He noticed.

She dropped her gaze to his bow tie, cheeks hot.

"Don't be embarrassed. It's always been like this between us. It's nice to see it's still there." He moved his touch to the arc above the necklace, tickling her collarbone, then slid his fingertip up her throat, lightly urging her chin to come up, forcing her gaze to lift to his. "I know you don't remember how good it is, but it is very, very good, Alexandra."

She did remember. It was.

Between her headaches and his cast and their different

sleep schedules, they'd been using separate bedrooms, but she yearned for the closeness they'd always enjoyed. She swept her lashes down so he wouldn't see how much, but she was very tempted to lean forward and tilt her mouth up to his.

"Come to me later if you want to. I would like that." He let his straying touch drop from the hollow beneath her ear and gathered his crutches under his arms.

Later. Not now. He always directed and she always obeyed. She was such a pushover where he was concerned.

That agitating thought turned an otherwise velvety evening into an irritation. The fading dusk became fully dark while they made their way to the museum, so she left her sunglasses in the car and regretted it as soon as they arrived inside. The chandeliers were dimmed, but there was a waterfall effect on one wall that she averted her gaze from studying.

The room was noisy, too. Full of glitterati who immediately noticed them. She didn't get a chance to ask for someone to retrieve her sunglasses. They were approached and she was forced to smile as people expressed their concern.

Rafael introduced her to a couple they already knew. "Alexandra is having trouble with her memory, but otherwise, we're recovering nicely."

"Really!" The woman's voice pitched high with astonishment. "You don't remember our shopping trip in Singapore? While our men were in meetings?"

"I don't." In truth, she was happy to forget this particular woman, especially when she took it upon herself to pass along Alexandra's condition to a mutual acquaintance the minute another couple joined them.

"Can you believe it? She doesn't recognize any of us."

She waved at Alexandra as though she was a curiosity, not a person.

Rafael stiffened beside her. "Such a shame, too," he said. "I'm sure she thought the world of you before this."

Oof. Not that she didn't appreciate his coming to her defense, but what had he thought would happen when they started sharing news like this?

She gritted her teeth, thinking it would be a long, painful night when he touched her elbow and said, "There's someone we need to speak to. Excuse us."

The gossipy woman's husband saved Sasha from what would have been a reaction of near violent startlement.

"Casella?" the man asked, looking past her. "That deal is going through, then?"

"Yes." As Rafael's gaze crashed back into hers, she was already gathering up her composure, ignoring the ringing in her ears as she turned to face Gio and…

Yes. That woman dressed like a golden goddess was Molly.

What the *hell*? Why hadn't Rafael warned her they would see them here? *He* didn't look surprised by their appearance.

"Who, um… Wasn't that the name of the man you said…" She frowned, feigning an attempt to place a name as she paced beside him. "I'm trying to remember what you said when you told me about the surrogate. That she was engaged to your business partner? That's not *her*, is it?"

"Molly. Yes," he said with a watchful look in her direction.

"Why didn't you warn me they would be here? Does he know she's—?"

"No."

"Then why—?" They were coming into earshot with the other couple.

Sasha's stomach tensed around a hot ember of anger as she looked for some avenue of escape while keeping a blank expression frozen to her face.

She couldn't risk Molly guessing that she still had her memory. The whole house of cards would come down. She tried to appear bored by this whole event, but she couldn't help studying her friend, searching for signs their baby was still safe inside her.

Molly's gown had an empire waist so any bump under that drape of silk was well disguised. Her ample breasts were likely all that people noticed, especially since they were adorned with the yellow sapphires of a dramatic necklace.

"Rafael. It's good to see you on your feet. Foot," Gio corrected wryly as he offered his hand. He wore a tuxedo with a black jacket and looked positively dashing. Really, it was no surprise that Molly would engage herself to him, not when he was that handsome and she'd already been nursing a crush.

"It's not slowing me down too much." Rafael dismissed his comment as he tucked his crutch beneath his armpit and shook Gio's hand. "And this must be your fiancée, Molly?"

"We've met. I was on your yacht last year, working for Gio. You may not remember." Molly sent questioning looks between the two of them, likely baffled by their silence since the crash.

"I don't remember anything," Sasha lied blatantly. "I have a concussion from the crash and lost all my memory." The farce of the moment was so acute, she could hardly keep her hysterical laughter from exploding out of her straining throat.

Molly gasped and expressed concern, but continued pretending she didn't know either of them, including all of Sasha's biggest and worst secrets. Rafael was acting as though Molly was someone he'd met once, not letting on that she was carrying their baby.

Sasha clung to her fake amnesia, but blurted, "These lights are giving me a headache. Rafael insisted on parading me around like I'm a circus attraction, but I'd like to leave."

Which was exactly what she did.

Rafael had learned his lesson. He waited until they were home before he said, "That was rude."

By then, Alexandra had taken a pain pill in the car and had put her sunglasses back on, but didn't seem to be wilting into a migraine.

"*I* was rude? You ambushed me!" She kicked off her heels and stalked down the hall to her room.

Yes, but, "I hoped that seeing her would shake something loose."

"Like my temper?" She swung her hair to the front of her shoulder and turned, pointing at her spine exactly the way she'd done a thousand times when they had undressed after an evening out. "I *thought* her surrogacy was supposed to be a secret. You said she signed an NDA. What was I supposed to say to her there? Hi, how's our baby cooking?"

"The secrecy is to keep your parents from finding out. If something had slipped out this evening, I don't think it would have got back to them." He lowered her zip.

As soon as the gown loosened, she caught it against her

breasts and swung around to confront him. "I can't trust you at all, can I?"

"You can trust me with your life, Alexandra. You already have."

She choked out a noise of disbelief and walked away, shedding the gown onto the floor and closing herself into the bathroom.

He pinched the bridge of his nose, accepting that it had been a bad move to not tell her, but he really had hoped it would jar her memory into coming back.

When she came out fifteen minutes later, her face was clean and she wore a white robe. She checked as she saw him.

"I should have warned you," he acknowledged. "But that's how I learned to play when I want something."

"Dirty?"

"Yes," he said without apology. "I want *you*, Alexandra. I want my wife back."

She studied him for a long time, mouth pouted in sorrow. Then sighed.

"I will never again be the woman you married. I need you to accept that, Rafael. If that's what you're holding out for, we should call it quits right now." Her somber, rational tone sent a preternatural shiver down his spine. A sort of panic.

"All right. It wasn't just your memory I was testing," he admitted. "I wanted to see your reaction to her." He wanted to pace, but his freaking leg was broken. He had to make do with sitting on the end of the bed and removing the jacket that was causing him to overheat. "It's childish, but I wanted to see if you had the same instant connection to her."

"What do you mean?" Only one lamp burned, but she picked up her sunglasses and put them on.

"I've never seen you take to anyone the way you reacted to her. I mean, I guess your reaction this evening was exactly the same as the first time you met her, since you were rude to her then, too." He tugged at his bow tie, thinking back to how odd that day had been. "You did a quick about-face and decided she ought to be our surrogate. That never made sense to me, but you seemed excited for the possibility so I went along with it. As things progressed, you became very close with her. I'm embarrassed to admit that it began to feel like an affair, even though you were only texting with her. She calls you Sasha."

"What's wrong with that?" She had her fists buried in the pockets of her robe. Her shoulders were hunched defensively.

"You've never invited me to call you anything but Alexandra." God, he felt puerile saying that.

"You can call me Sasha if you want to." She wasn't pandering. She was frowning behind her sunglasses. "Alexandra feels like a stranger who is carrying a lot of other people's expectations. That's what Winnie called me. I kind of hate being Alexandra."

I will never again be the woman you married.

He *would* have to accept that. In fact, everything about their marriage was shifting, partly due to her memory loss, but also because of the baby.

"I'm going to connect with Molly tomorrow." Hopefully without Gio. He should have tried harder to speak with her this evening, to gauge their relationship, but he'd been more concerned about his wife's reaction than the deal he had yet to finalize.

Damn. That was sobering to acknowledge.

"What will you say to her?" she asked warily.

"I'll find out where things stand. Our arrangement was that she would leave her employment by now and stay at the island estate for the rest of her pregnancy. She had talked about your staying there with her. Would you?" he asked, subconsciously bracing for the answer.

She nodded jerkily, mouth pensive. "Yes. I'd like that."

Damn. That felt...bad.

Shortly after their marriage, when Sasha had gained access to the first portion of her fortune, Rafael had suggested this island estate as a good investment. Humbolt had played the stock market—poorly—and invested wherever it served his attempts to be part of the old boys' club.

Sasha had received a lot of her trust in properties, several of which she had sold out of spite, so her mother couldn't use them, but also so she could buy this.

It consisted of a modern villa amid sprawling acres of farmland that not only paid for itself, but produced a profit off the sale of oranges, olives, lamb, and wine. She had fallen in love with it and only wished they had more time to spend here.

Now was her chance, she thought privately, as Rafael showed her and Molly around.

The property gave the impression of being remote, situated up a hill with a view overlooking the sea, but it was a relatively short helicopter ride back to Athens, should Molly need attention. There was also a nearby village where a nurse-midwife had a small practice. It was already arranged that she would come by tomorrow and continue checking on both women regularly. A housekeeper would come by three times a week with groceries and whatever else they might need.

Sasha knew all of this since she had arranged it, but she paid attention as though it was new information. After nearly three weeks of this game, she was clinging to her lie by her fingernails.

Molly thanked Rafael, then excused herself to the powder room. Talk about a pretense! That woman was *definitely* showing. Sasha had about a thousand questions for her, all of them around her relationship with Gio, but she walked Rafael out to the helipad first.

"Maybe wear a hat when you go outside," he said as he searched through the lenses of her sunglasses. "Are you sure you don't want the housekeeper to move in full-time?"

"No, we'll manage." Sasha dug deep to keep this bland look on her face, so he wouldn't know how close she was to breaking.

"All right. I'll—" He released a hiss of pent-up frustration. "I'll try to come back next weekend, but now that Gio has pulled the pin, I have a lot of triage in front of me."

Sasha had yet to get the full story on *that*, too.

Rafael surprised her by ducking his head and stealing a brief, hard kiss that turned the embers of her old yearnings into a conflagration of instant need.

She had barely reacted before he was pulling away, leaving her breathless as he swung on his crutches toward the helicopter.

She stepped backward into the shade, but didn't step inside until the rotors began to turn. Then she watched from the window as the helicopter lifted off, taking him back to Athens. She felt rather bereft as he became a dot in the sky and disappeared.

When she turned away from the glass, Molly was hovering in the archway between the lounge and the kitchen.

"Oh, don't look so stressed out, Moll. I'm faking. The only memory I lost was the actual crash."

"What? Oh, my *Gawd*, Sasha. Why would you do that?" she cried.

Sasha winced one eye closed and patted the air. "My concussion is real and so are the headaches. Keep your voice down."

"Sorry," Molly whispered and tiptoed closer. "But what on earth?"

"I was trying to get rid of my parents. It got out of hand. And things with Rafael became *impossible*. I love him *so much* and he doesn't feel the same." Her eyes began to well with tears of hurt and despair.

Molly, bless her, didn't judge. In fact, her face crumpled.

"I love Gio, too. I told him last night. This morning we had a fight about it. Then he caught me with Rafael and thought I'd been having an affair with him. Rafael explained this is your baby, too, which was hard enough for Gio to wrap his head around. I couldn't tell him *why* I wanted to carry your baby. He thinks it's only for the money, and there are things in his past that make him look down on me for th-that..."

"Oh, Moll." Sasha rushed over to hug her friend. They both fell apart.

Molly held on to her really tight and choked through her sobs, "I'm not sorry, though. Okay? I don't regret anything about doing this. Nothing," she stressed, then mumbled into Sasha's hair, "Except the part where we've checked into Heartbreak Hotel together."

"Really?" Sasha drew back a little. "There's no one else I'd rather be miserable with."

They both sputtered into teary laughter.

Rafael felt like a guest when he entered the villa a week later.

Molly came from the kitchen with a tray of glasses and a pitcher of lemonade. She wore a simple cotton sundress that draped from a high waist to curtain her bump. Her brown hair was in a ponytail. Her face and feet were bare, making her look about fifteen years old.

"Shall we sit by the pool? Sasha's on a video call upstairs, but she'll have heard the helicopter. I'm sure she'll be down shortly."

"Who is she chatting with?" He glanced with dismay at the spiral staircase. He was moving better on these sticks, but would break his neck trying to negotiate those see-through steps.

"Dr. Narula suggested we reconnect with our counselor."

"Is she having trouble bonding with the baby?" he asked with alarm, following her out the doors to the shaded part of the terrace.

"I wouldn't say that. But I don't want to speak for her," she added with an apologetic smile. "Also…" She hesitated, then said plainly, "We talk about a lot of things, but there are things we don't talk about. You, for instance. We only talk about you in very general terms. She told me that you've both had some ups and downs as a result of the fertility troubles, but she doesn't go into detail. I thought you'd like to know she doesn't gossip about you."

"Hmph." He sat and half drained the icy lemonade she handed him. "How are you? How's the baby?"

"The nurse was here yesterday. No concerns." She patted her middle, smiling.

"But you're also speaking to the counselor? Are you having misgivings?"

"Not at all. But after what happened that day with Gio…" Her brow crinkled. "I knew having this baby would change my life, but I thought I could go back to my old life afterward. Now I know that's not going to happen. I wanted to talk that out with her. Have you, um—" She peered at him, asking with a cringe of apprehension, "Have you spoken to Gio?"

"No." Gio had been murderous when he had caught them together. He had leaped to the correct conclusion that his secretary-fiancée was carrying Rafael's baby. The part where the baby was also Sasha's had put him into a tailspin.

Sasha. Rafael had begun thinking of his wife by that name, feeling closer to her when he did.

Molly was staring at him like a puppy waiting for a bite of cheese so he pulled his mind back to their conversation.

"My people have reached out, but he's not answering. I'm sure it will be fine." He didn't believe that at all, but he didn't want to drop a guilt trip on her.

Molly had kept their secret right up until the showdown in the suite. She swore that Gio would keep the fact the baby was theirs confidential, but Rafael wasn't as certain. He'd seen the dark side of humanity. He knew how useful this type of leverage could be for a man like Gio and was working night and day, ensuring that Gio couldn't use this to damage him.

"If you need a job after this, tell me. I'll find you a place," he assured Molly.

"Thank you, but it's not about needing a job. I won't

have to work for a long time, thanks to your generosity." She traced a finger through the dew on her glass, brow crinkling. "It's more that I'm the type who likes to know what's coming. Now my future is a big ol' white space. But after the baby comes, I'll spend some time with my mom and sister. That will be good. It will all work out."

He wondered if that practical optimism and quiet confidence was what Sasha liked about her. It was very appealing.

"How are you and Sasha getting along?" he asked.

"Good. Ah, here she is. I knew she would have heard the helicopter. I'll leave you two to catch up." Molly rose with undisguised haste. She faltered briefly as she passed Sasha and waited for Sasha to nod before she entered the house and closed the door.

Rafael noted that Sasha held a tissue in her fist and tried to see past the black cat's eye lenses she wore. "Have you been crying?"

"I was talking to the counselor." She shoved the tissue under her nose. Her mood seemed heavy. Her hair was loose, she wore no lipstick, and her sundress was a simple thing with spaghetti straps and a flecked print of yellow on green. She was still the most beautiful woman he'd ever seen.

"About the baby?" he asked, bracing himself.

"About…" She sighed and said, "There's usually a breeze out at the gazebo by this time of day. Can you walk that far?"

The path was hard-packed gravel so he easily managed it.

"Another week and I should have a walking cast," he said when they arrived in the shaded octagon where there was, in fact, a very nice breeze. There was also a pair of daybeds. The table between held a stack of paperback romances, sunscreen, a hair tie, and the start of some knitting in a buttery yellow yarn.

He leaned on a post so he could study Sasha's profile while she stood at the rail, facing the sea.

"How are things here?"

"Good." She brightened. "Molly felt the baby move. I didn't yet, but we keep trying."

A pang went through him, partly made up of that sense of threat he experienced when she was close with their surrogate, but the anticipation in her face was such a relief, he could only be pleased by this development.

"You're feeling good about the baby?" he prompted. "Less worried?"

"A little." She immediately plunged back to pensive, chewing the corner of her mouth.

"Do you want to tell me about the counselor?" he asked.

"There's a lot to unpack, but the biggest issue is...." Her brow wrinkled with real distress. "I don't know how to make this marriage work if you don't..." Her voice withered.

Don't love me?

Everything in him became gripped with tension. Was he incapable of love? Or merely afraid of it? Maybe if they had weathered the infertility storm without it causing such a rift between them, he might have allowed himself to be more vulnerable with her, but the more she had distanced herself, the less able he'd been to bridge that gap. He was beginning to see that now. Once Molly had come into the picture, he had put up even more walls.

"If you don't know who I really am," she finished in a shaken voice.

It took him a moment for his brain to catch up. Her words pulled him out of his introspection into seeing an easy fix. "I don't blame you for not knowing who you are. I'm enjoying getting to know you. Sasha."

Her gaze flashed to his. "That's the first time you've called me that."

"Do you mind?"

"No." Her voice thickened. "I like hearing it in your voice."

That hit him like such a heart punch he couldn't breathe. Then he noticed her mouth was quivering as though she was on the verge of tears again.

"What's wrong?"

She looked at her hands. "I wish everything could be… where it needs to be, between us. That we didn't have to go through fire to get there. I don't know if we'll survive it."

"Hey." He leaned out and grazed her hand with his fingertips. "Come here."

She warily placed her fingers into his palm, allowing him to tug her closer.

"We have time. Even once the baby is here, we can take as long as you need." He brought her hand to his mouth and kissed her knuckle. "Time is being forced upon us, actually."

"What do you mean?"

"I have some leads in Asia and Australia. Gio is stonewalling. He hasn't dissolved the deal, but he won't finalize it, either. I have to put contingency plans in place, so I'm leaving for a few weeks. I was going to ask you to come with me, but I can see how important it is for you to be here. That it's helping you feel closer to our baby."

"It is, but…" Her fingers clenched onto his and her mouth seemed to search for words.

He wished he could see the beckoning blue of her eyes.

"But you'll miss me?" he suggested, inviting her closer by guiding her hand up to the back of his neck.

She flowed into him and he dipped his head to kiss her as naturally as he always had.

When her other hand splayed against his rib cage, he paused, but she wasn't pressing in protest. She roamed her palm against his side, then slid her hand around to his back, leaning into him until her curves were flat against his front.

His brain turned inside out.

He let his crutches fall and grasped at the rail to keep himself firmly on his feet while he hooked his other hand behind her neck, dragging her that inch closer so he could kiss her the way he'd been needing to since she'd awakened in Rome and stared at him as though he was a stranger.

A jolt of surprise went through her, then she moaned into his mouth and melted against him. One hand went up to the back of his head, where her fingers sifted into his hair. The one at his back slid down to massage his ass.

His body's response—the sliding tension through his abdomen and the pour of heat into his groin—was stronger than ever.

Her lips opened to invite an even hungrier kiss. He ravaged her, thinking only one thought. How could anything part them when they had *this*? The precariousness between them fell away. Here, with the taste of her intoxicating him, here everything was right and solid and *good*.

When she pressed her hips into his in the most exquisite way, as though she remembered exactly how much he liked that crushing space between pleasure and pain, he groaned and dropped his hand to her tailbone, encouraging the roll of her hips.

She was on her tiptoes, one long, lithe line against him. He wanted to fill his hands with her. Kneel and lavish her with his tongue. He wanted to press her to one of those daybeds and meld them together for all time.

He couldn't do any of those things, not with this damned cast.

He gripped the rail with all his strength and encouraged the rhythm of their grinding hips. The soft cheek of her ass filled his palm and her breasts rubbed his chest and her breath shortened.

This lovely, lovely woman was bringing him to the brink, seeking the pressure of his diamond-hard erection against her mound. Mewing into his mouth. Tensing.

Just when he thought he would explode like a teenager, she shuddered and dropped her head back to release small cries of joy into the rafters above them.

As her whole body went limp, he released her ass— he'd probably left a handprint there—and cradled his arm around her, holding her up while he inhaled the sweet smell of her hair and the knowledge that he could still bring her off without either of them getting undressed.

"I thought…" Her voice was unsteady. She wedged her arms between them. "I thought you were with me."

"I nearly was." His voice was thick with the lust that still coursed through him. He let his hand trace up and down her spine. "But edging myself while making you come is pretty much my favorite pastime."

"I don't understand."

"It's when—"

"I know what edging is," she muttered. "Which one of us are you controlling? Me or you?"

"Both. It's fun to see how long I can last. I didn't think this one through, of course. I'm going to be horny for weeks."

She made a noise of amusement, but her mouth was pouted in thought.

He was starting to resent those sunglasses and the way they made it so hard to read what was going on behind them.

"Help me to that daybed and I'll let you break me," he invited, voice rasped with anticipation.

"No," she scolded, chin dipping so he could only see the crown of her head where her dirty blond roots were coming in. Still, her head canted as she looked toward the bed, as though she was gauging the distance and thinking about it.

"Why not? Worried Molly will see us? It's below the rail." The crisscrossed slats provided a screen that allowed the breeze to float across the lower half of the gazebo but left the beds in shadow. "Or because you don't remember doing it to me before? Because you have."

Tension invaded her that wasn't all sexual. It was reluctance. Resistance?

"Sasha."

Her head came up, startled.

"We don't have to. It's fine." Horniness wasn't terminal. It only felt that way. He cupped her cheek. "But I want you to know that the first time we made love, we were complete strangers. We didn't even know each other's names."

Her lips parted, then tilted between naughty humor and something that struck him as rueful. His heart swerved.

"Do you remember that?"

"What? No." She stepped away and bent to pick up his crutches. "Are you staying for dinner? It's Molly's night to cook. We should let her know if you are."

Slowly, Sasha was coming to terms with things she should have addressed years ago. Or, rather, she was beginning to believe what she had known in her head but hadn't been able to accept in her heart. Her affair with a married man hadn't been her fault. Her "lover" had exploited a troubled teenager and played the victim when his actions had consequences.

Deciding to keep her pregnancy a secret, then placing Libby with Patty, had been the only real agency she'd had at the time. She had taken control of her circumstance and her future to the best of her ability. She shouldn't feel ashamed of the decisions she'd made.

Sometimes she even listened to Molly talk to Libby and felt really good about what she'd done.

Then Molly came out to where she was lazing by the pool and announced starkly, "That was Mom. Gio went to see her. He was looking at family photos and figured it out, Sash. He knows you're Libby's birth mom."

"What?" She sat up, scrambling to keep her sunglasses in place. "Rafael can't hear that from someone else."

"Gio won't say anything. Mom impressed on him that it's not his place. I genuinely don't believe he would do that to Libby. He's met her during our chats and seems to like her. He's not malicious."

Even so, the possibility of being outed hung like a storm cloud over her.

The next time she spoke to Rafael, she asked when he would be home.

"I'll be here at least another week. I was able to get my cast off so at least one thing is going in my favor. Why? Do you miss me?"

She hesitated, surprised at the question, no matter how cocky he'd sounded as he delivered it. He had never asked for confirmations of affection in the past.

But they had started having much deeper conversations, especially now that they were apart. She talked to him about the baby and her growing excitement for its arrival. He said he wished one of his mothers had lived to meet her grandchild.

One night, she asked him why he was so determined to expand his father's business.

"Spite," he replied.

She still couldn't use screens, so his voice was in her ear, and maybe that was why he filled the silence that she deliberately left for him to continue.

"The day my father died, I came into the office to find the local gang roughing him up. He couldn't breathe. I got into it with them and was on the floor myself when I realized he had collapsed from more than a gut punch. They took my phone and yanked out the landlines. I went to three different businesses, but none would call an ambulance. They'd been there ahead of me, intimidating them against helping us."

"That's horrible."

"It was. By the time I got an ambulance to him, he was

gone. But I wasn't," he said with grit. "And I made sure they knew it."

The growing openness between them gave her the courage to admit, "Yes. I do miss you."

Every time she spoke to him, she thought, *Come home.*

"I miss you, too. I wish you were here." He sounded tired and maybe something else that she couldn't quite put her finger on. Homesick? "You always charm people's socks off."

"Including yours?" It was a lilt of flirtation she tossed out to lift him from his brooding.

"They're already off," he retorted. "I'm fresh out of the shower wearing only a towel. Why? What are you wearing?" The way his voice dipped into smoky and wicked sent a pulse of temptation deep between her thighs.

She swallowed. "Just a sundress."

"Just?"

"And underwear."

"Are you in your room? Alone?"

She glanced out the window to see Molly was at the gazebo. She hurried up the stairs to her bedroom. "I am now," she said, breathless from more than the climb.

"Don't lock the door. Lean against it and take off your underwear, but leave them around your ankles."

"Why?" she asked, prickling with nervous excitement.

"Because I want you to open your legs as far as you can and imagine my hands are cuffing your ankles. I'm kneeling in front of you and I'm going to lick your fingers as you caress yourself. Tell me when you start doing that."

"What, um…" She felt jittery and naughty and aroused as she let the scrap of lace drop. "What are you doing?"

"Opening my towel and thinking I won't be so selfless this time. I'm going to come when you do."

"Oh." She pressed the back of her head to the hard door.

"Are you touching yourself? Tell me *exactly* what you're doing," he prompted in a velvety voice that rasped across her senses. "I'll tell you exactly what *I'm* doing while I'm there on the floor in front of you."

Her husband had a really filthy mouth, but she seemed to possess a kinky streak that liked it. Within a few minutes, her helpless sobs were filling the room. He owned her, he really did, even from nine thousand miles away.

But as his groan of completion resounded in her ear, her panting lips curved into a tender smile. She felt close to him, despite the distance. She really did.

"When I finally get my hands on you, we won't leave our bed for a week," he promised in a voice she knew very well. It was the one that often played against her ear when she was basking in this same afterglow.

It dimmed as she waited to find out if Gio would use what he knew, but as time wore on she began to believe Gio really would stay silent about Libby.

Then Rafael called one morning to say, "I rerouted to Genoa."

"What?" she cried. "I thought you were coming to Athens."

"Gio Casella finally picked up the phone."

"I was going to come see you." She had only been toying with the idea, but panic had the words blurting out of her.

"I would love that," he said in a throaty voice. "But if he actually goes through with signing the contract, it will be an all-hands situation while I finally get everything off the ground. I want to give you my full attention once we're together so I'll come to you when I can."

Wait, she thought, but he ended the call.

CHAPTER TEN

HE SIGNED IT.

Gio didn't need this partnership as badly as Rafael did, but if he walked away from this deal, he knew Rafael would find someone else and compete against him. He was a practical businessman so he got over his snit and closed the deal.

Rafael had braced himself for fresh haggling and threats to expose the surrogacy arrangement, but Gio only adjusted some dates to reflect the time they'd lost. He remained frosty, though, not mentioning Molly's name or asking how she was doing.

That didn't surprise Rafael. Apparently, their engagement had been a sham, but Rafael was offended on her behalf and said as much before he left. Probably not his smartest move, but he liked her and thought Gio should have treated her better.

The deal was done, though, creating a proverbial electric fence around his own assets. The growth would be exponential and, yes, he would have achieved his nine zeroes well before the age of thirty-five, which was the goal he had set for himself.

That should have brought him more satisfaction than it did. He hurried back to Athens to get things moving, but he was only irritated by the mountain of meetings and decisions that landed on him. He was usually energized by this type of thing, but all he could think about was carving out time to see his wife.

By the time he was finally on his way to see her, they had been nearly two months apart. This house wasn't a home without her and he wanted her here. She had even offered to come to him, but he wanted to collect her. At twenty-four weeks, the baby was moving enough that he might feel one of those kicks for himself.

Since when had he become a family man? Next, he'd be falling in love.

He paused in changing out of his suit to consider that.

His priorities had definitely shifted, which felt unfamiliar, but not as alarming as it might have a year or even a few months ago.

Sasha's memory loss was still a concern, of course, but they were finding their way out of the rough patch that had plagued them for so long. In some ways, her amnesia served them. It had forced them to set aside their go-to coping strategy of lust—notwithstanding the phone sex—and address the underlying issues they had ignored. He had had to name those issues for her and acknowledge his role in their various mistakes. Things like his remoteness and refusal to share his most difficult memories.

Letting her in felt risky as hell, but he understood that trust was a two-way street. He had to offer it to gain it, so he was letting down his guard with her. She was still a mystery to herself as well as him, but he was getting to know her all over again and, to his eternal delight, was more attracted to her than ever. She was softer these days. More vulnerable.

He felt more protective of her than ever and couldn't

wait until they were finally together, with their baby, in their home again.

Her name came up on his phone and he slid to accept the call.

"I know, I know," he said. "I'm grabbing a few things from the house, then I'll—"

"Molly's bleeding," she said starkly. "The nurse is here and the helicopter is on its way. We'll meet you at the hospital in Athens."

"Is the baby—?"

"I don't *know*, Rafael. I don't know why this keeps happening! Why am I not allowed to have a baby?" Her anguish was knife-sharp and ripened by fear, but the words and the old defeat baked within them sent a cold flush through his body.

"Alexandra." He wasn't consciously aware of grasping at that old name, but he instinctively knew that's who he was talking to. "Do you have your memories back?"

"They never left," she cried. "I *tried* to forget, but—"

"You remember everything? You've been lying to me all this time?" It was such a crack in the face, it should have knocked his own memories into another universe.

"Rafael." Her tone pulled back from hysteria.

"No," he said, because he couldn't accept it. Not right now. Not when their baby was in jeopardy. "I'll meet you at the hospital."

He ended the call, so blind with outrage he couldn't form a thought or move a muscle.

"Sir?" Tino asked, reminding him that his assistant had been hovering this whole time. "I heard 'hospital.' Is there something I can do?"

That kicked Rafael's sluggish brain into gear.

"Yes. Tell the driver we're going into the city, not the helipad." He gave him the name of the hospital Molly would be flown to.

Her mother. Somehow his scattered thoughts snagged on the importance of informing Molly's mother.

Rafael wasted precious minutes flicking through old emails until he found her number.

Patricia sounded distracted when she picked up.

"It's Rafael, Alexandra's husband. I wanted to let you know that Molly is on her way to the hospital—"

"I just got off the phone with Gio," Patricia cut in. Tension was evident beneath her firmly controlled tone. "He's in New York and has arranged a flight for us. We're leaving the house right now. He said we should be there in twelve hours or so."

Gio. How the hell had *he* heard about this? Molly? It didn't matter. Patricia and Molly's sister were on their way. That was all that mattered.

"I'll update you at this number?" Rafael asked.

"Thank you. We'll see you soon."

She was a midwife, he recalled. She was likely used to medical emergencies, but not ones that involved her daughter.

Guilt assailed him along with profound worry. He didn't know Molly well, but he liked her. He had to wonder, however, whether *she* knew that his wife had been lying to him all this time?

He would bet any money that she did, given how close she was to Sasha. The thought made him even more furious, filling him with such a sense of betrayal he could barely function.

He stewed all the way into the city. Molly had just arrived when he did. She was being assessed so he was directed to a private lounge.

Alexandra was already there. She wore one of her casual sundresses that buttoned from its square neckline down to her knees. A drawstring at her waist gave it a figure-hugging shape, but it was crushed and one of the buttons had slipped free.

She was ghostly white and froze when she saw him.

Conflicting impulses rocketed through him. He had an instinct to rush forward and comfort her. To comfort himself with the solace of her willowy body leaning into his. Getting to twenty-four weeks had made this seem like a sure thing. To have the rug pulled at this stage would be devastating.

At the same time, he was so angry with her, so bitterly disgusted, he could hardly look at her.

"Your cast is gone."

"I told you it was off. What happened? To Molly," he clarified. "Did she fall?"

"No. Nothing. She felt fine. A little tired, but only because the baby woke her early with a big k-kick." Her voice hiccuped. "We were talking. She was upset about Gio, but she was just a bit weepy, not… Anyway, she stood up and we realized she was bleeding."

Her hand shook as she wiped beneath her seeping eye.

"I called for the helicopter, then the nurse. She flew in with us. She thinks it could be a placental abruption. That's when…" Her voice faded with a fear so visceral, it made the hairs on his arms stand up. "When the placenta p-pulls away…"

"I understand." He couldn't bear it. He might want to shout himself hoarse at her, but he couldn't see straight.

This was their *baby*. He crossed to her in a few lurching strides and yanked her against his chest.

She shuddered and clung to him, catching back sobs.

They stood a long time like that, clinging to each other as though cast away at sea. They clung to hope, not relaxing their grip until the doctor came in and confirmed the nurse's suspicion.

"The baby's vitals are strong and Molly's bleeding has subsided, but we'll keep her here on strict bed rest and monitor her closely. Hopefully, we can buy a week or two, but she will deliver early. We've started her on steroids to help the baby's lungs develop. We've also given her a mild pain reliever so she'll be drowsy when you see her. They're settling her in her room now. It won't be much longer."

"Can I ask you to speak with Molly's mother?" Rafael asked the doctor. "She's on her way here, but I'm sure she's anxious for news." He gave the doctor Patricia's number and the doctor left to make that call.

"Thank you. I don't know that I could have repeated any of that," Sasha said.

Or should he call her Alexandra? He didn't know who he was talking to anymore! He felt raw, absolutely peeled down to his core that she had lied to him so cold-bloodedly. For so long, too.

He had known she was capable of deception, but not like this. Not something directed at him. It made her seem like a stranger all over again. Like their whole marriage had been one long lie.

At the same time, she was exactly the woman he knew as she absently pulled the tie from her hair, then gathered it into a fresh bun to resecure it. He'd seen her do that so many times it was imprinted on him as *her*.

"Did Molly call Gio to bring them?" he asked.

"I did. You hung up on me," she reminded him flatly. "And—" She looked with frustration between the kettle and single-cup coffee maker. "God, I could use a drink. I know you're angry about…what I did."

"I'm angry that you enlisted Gio to do something that was my responsibility," he said stiffly. "'Angry' doesn't begin to describe how I feel about you lying to my face for two straight months. Is that what really turned you on while we were having all that phone sex?"

She stared at him through a long, drawn-out moment of silence, then blinked once in a way that was decidedly withering, but her voice shook as she said, "No, Rafael. I don't get off on power the way you do."

"Kýrie and Kyría Zamos?" A nurse poked her head into the lounge. "Kyría Brooks can see you now, but only for a moment. She needs to rest."

Molly was on her side in the hospital bed, various tubes and wires emerging from beneath the blankets that covered her.

"Moll?" Sasha brushed her hair off her face with such tender familiarity, it struck a knife into Rafael's heart. "You doing okay, pal?"

"Mmm-hmm." She left her eyes shut. "Baby's okay, too, but they're going to keep me."

"I know. Your mom is on her way."

Molly's eye opened. "With Lib?"

Sasha nodded, mouth pressed into a grave line. "Yes. It's okay. I think it will be."

Molly's somber gaze shifted to Rafael.

"I haven't told him yet, but I will," Sasha said.

Molly's arm wormed its way out from beneath the

blanket. She wiggled her fingers at Rafael, beckoning him closer.

"I know you're mad at me, too, but…" She reached out farther, insisting he give her his hand.

When he did, she guided his palm to press against the side of her bump. It was a surprisingly firm curve. Through the layer of cotton and the warmth of her body, he felt the slightest nudge against his palm.

His breath was kicked clean out of him.

He swung his awe-filled gaze to his wife and caught such a look of envy and sorrow on her face, it was another punch to the gut. She wanted to be the one to give him this. He knew that. She might have lied about other things, but her desire to have this baby was real.

She hid her torment behind a faint smile, then pointed at Molly's phone on the bedside table.

"Call if you need me. We have an apartment a few blocks away. I'll come back when Patty lands."

"Okay," Molly murmured, blinking sleepily. "It's going to be okay, Sash."

"I know," Sasha said, but when she looked up at Rafael, there was nothing but hell in her eyes. She knew as well as he did that they stood to lose everything.

Including each other.

The apartment in Athens was a one-bedroom flat they kept stocked for occasions when they had a late night in the city.

While Rafael set out some takeout he'd picked up, Sasha pulled on a pair of soft joggers and a long-sleeved shirt, chilled to the bone by the air-conditioning that was staving off the still-hot September temperatures.

She knocked back a shot of ouzo on her way to the table

before accepting the glass of white wine Rafael poured her. Absolutely nothing in her was interested in the souvlaki skewers he plated.

"I was going to tell you when you came back to the island, but you went to Asia—"

"And there was no possible way you could have told me over the phone," he said coldly. "Or simply *told the truth* when I asked you in Rome."

Heaviness sat on her heart. It was the heaviness of earned guilt.

"I know I'm in the wrong. I know you'll have a hard time forgiving me, but... You laughed at me, Rafael." The mere mention of it still caused a piercing sensation in the middle of her chest.

"When?" He was ignoring his own meal, pacing with a slight limp, but otherwise back to being the dynamic man she'd married—severely handsome and so muscled and powerful, his stiff shoulders strained the fabric of his shirt.

"When I told you I loved you."

"No, I didn't."

"You did. I said I loved you and you said you thought I was going to say I love Molly. Then you *laughed.*"

"At myself. For thinking that," he said impatiently. "That doesn't excuse your making a fool of me ever since!"

"That's not why I did it," she said wearily. "That's why it started. Actually, I was screwing with my parents and it snowballed from there. I—" She made herself stop pacing. Stop trying to find rationalizations.

Stop running from the past.

She turned to face him. She faced all of it head-on.

"When I was sixteen, one of Humbolt's friends seduced me. I got pregnant and ran away to have the baby. I lived with Molly and her mom. They adopted her. Molly's sister, Libby, is my daughter."

He stood so still she didn't think he was even breathing.

She swallowed and folded her arms around herself.

"That's why I was so upset when I couldn't get pregnant. I did it before without even trying. I should have been able to do it again."

"Why didn't you tell me that?"

"I couldn't make the words come out of my mouth." That was the truth, but not the whole truth. She took a shaken breath. "I buried that secret because it hurt, Rafael. It hurt so much that I couldn't look at it myself, let alone show it to you. We didn't share secrets. You said you were fond of me, but was that fondness going to hold up under knowing your wife had an affair with a married man? One with small children at home?"

"He had kids? How old was he?"

"Thirty-one."

"And you were sixteen? That's not an affair, Alexandra."

She flinched, hating to hear him call her that after he'd begun sounding so tender when he called her by her nickname.

"I know, but it wasn't against my will, either. I didn't fight him off. I thought I was in love. Mostly I loved the idea that screwing Humbolt's friend would get under Humbolt's skin. All I really did was give him a reason to call me a whore, though." She rubbed her eyebrow.

"He knew about it? And didn't put a stop to it?" He sounded murderous. "What about your mother?"

"She would never admit she knew. And that's not the point. I got pregnant, but I was a minor. I knew Humbolt would use my baby against me. Maybe they would have made me give it up anyway. Or my mother would have undercut my parenting to turn my child into yet another vapid socialite. Nothing about bringing that baby home would have worked in my favor or the baby's."

"That's the real reason you ran away back then. To have the baby."

She nodded. "Patty took me in and helped me hire a lawyer who got Libby's father to relinquish paternity rights. He also set up a trust for her, but I'm not allowed to reveal he's her father. That's another reason I had to keep the whole thing secret. If the paparazzi learned I'd had a baby, they would go digging. At least the fear that he could be exposed made Libby's father keep Humbolt in check to some extent."

"He didn't keep you out of a psych ward, though, did he? They should both be arrested!"

"You're right. But so many people would suffer if this came out now. Believe me, I've thought about it, but Libby's life would be overturned, not to mention the lives of her father's other children. They're not much older than she is. They don't deserve to be hounded by the press while their parents go through an ugly divorce. Maybe he would try to undo the trust. Humbolt would definitely go after Patty for harboring me. He'd ruin her career, likely make a play for custody of Libby since she's Mom's granddaughter and entitled to a slice of my fortune. I doubt he'd win, but the point would be the pain he caused along the way."

He swore under his breath, then used his hand to scrub across his face.

She didn't know what reaction she expected. Maybe some sort of absolution? Understanding, at least?

The weight of his silence sat like a ten-ton boulder on her heart. They hadn't stood a chance, she realized. Not given all that she'd been hiding. Not when he was a man who had never been taught to trust and she had betrayed the little trust he'd started to place in her.

"That's everything?" he asked with scowl of distrust.

"Yes. The only other thing I ever lie about is my weight when we fly."

"I always tell them to add a few kilos anyway," he muttered with distraction.

"A *few*?" That was literally the meanest thing he'd ever said to her.

"You could have told me this anytime," he said tightly. "Long before this." He swept his hand through the air.

"When, Rafael?" she asked with more defeat than challenge. "When you asked me to have your baby and I thought you'd divorce me if I refused?"

"I never said that."

"It was implied. When we married, you told me you needed an heir. I *wanted* a baby. I want our baby." She waved in the direction of the hospital, trying not to think about how precarious their baby's life was at this moment. "I didn't expect it to become so hard to make one. You take care of everything and I had one job, but I couldn't do it. I was too ashamed to tell you why I felt like I was being punished—"

"No." He shook his head. "You—"

"No, *listen*," she insisted. "For once. Please. When I saw Molly on the yacht, I couldn't even let her tell me about Libby. It was really hard for me to come this far, to be able to tell you about her, but that's because I never had any trust in our marriage in the first place. I didn't trust *you*."

He sucked in a breath as though taking another body blow.

"I've wanted to tell you so many times, but even when

we both nearly died and I asked you if we loved each other, you said that was never part of our deal. Why the hell would I share anything so deeply personal with you after that? I ran away the only way I could, by pretending I couldn't remember anything. I thought that would get us to a clean divorce, but you started telling me things I never knew. Things about *us*. Do you know how many times I thought we were engaged in all-out war when we have sex, because I thought you got off on controlling me? I didn't know you get off on holding yourself back."

"Are you serious?" His jaw went slack.

"And those phone calls, while you were away? I thought you were wooing me. That we were finally growing closer. But I knew it would blow up when I told you I had never really lost my memory so I put off telling you. I know that's wrong. I know it is. But I couldn't stay in the marriage we had. And I don't know how we can stay married now, but—" She began to choke up as fresh anxiety welled in her chest. "Can we— Can we have a truce and not make any decisions until we know—"

She couldn't break down in front of him.

"I need to lie down." She hurried into the bedroom and shut the door.

Rafael started to go after her, but heard the lock click. He sighed and looked at the forgotten drink in his hand.

He wanted to get hammered out of his mind, but he set the glass aside, too stunned to form a coherent thought. What the hell had he just heard?

His mind began to flicker with random memories that he reevaluated as they came and went. The way Sasha had reacted to Molly arriving on the yacht. The way she had stiffened once, when Rafael had asked Molly about her sister. Molly had spoken with enthusiasm and affection while Sasha had listened politely, but he had sensed something was off.

He remembered their wedding day, when there'd been a handful of strangers present, assembled to celebrate Sasha's engagement to someone else. There'd been a man there who had watched Sasha in a way that had made her set her jaw at a defiant angle. Rafael had hated him on sight and only remembered him because he'd instinctively filed him under "enemies" in his mental register.

He remembered Sasha's agitation when Molly's pregnancy had been confirmed and the way she'd broken down at the twelve-week scan. He had put it all down to her fertility struggles. She was entitled to some ambivalence, he'd thought, but he hadn't had any real idea of the things she'd been through.

He hadn't tried to find out, either.

I didn't feel safe telling you these things.

Talk about shame. He prided himself on looking after her well, but he hadn't. Not in the way that counted most.

On the other hand, if she had *loved* him, as she had said she did, how could she lie to him about her memory loss? She had been angry with him. Fine. But she had kept it up for two *months*. That started to feel like the opposite of love. A grudge.

He was exhausted, but he stayed on his feet, brooding, not realizing he was waiting until he heard her stir a few hours later.

She came out of the bedroom still wearing the clothes she'd changed into when they had arrived. She faltered when she saw he was also still awake.

"They've landed. They're on the way to the hospital." She kicked into a pair of sandals and collected her purse.

He picked up the keys to drive her, not bothering to ask if she wanted him to. They didn't speak again until he was coming out of the underground parking lot.

"My sunglasses," she muttered as she dug through her handbag.

He pulled his own from the compartment beside his visor and handed them to her.

"Thank you."

When they arrived, they were asked to wait in the lounge. Molly was asleep, but her mother and Libby had been allowed to step in to see her. Gio had also been relegated to the lounge. His face and clothes were lined by travel, or was that worry putting tension around his eyes?

Rafael nodded curtly. Their last two interactions had been chilly. All of their communications around their partnership were being handled by their various executive teams.

"Did, um, Patty tell—" Sasha started to ask Gio.

"She did." He nodded once.

"*He* knew?" Rafael couldn't help that his temperature immediately spiked again.

"He figured it out a few weeks ago, after visiting Patty," Sasha said defensively.

Weeks. "Before our meeting?" Rafael directed that at Gio.

Gio hitched a shoulder.

There was no comfort in knowing that Gio could have revealed Sasha's secrets and destroyed Rafael in twenty different ways. Instead, he had signed off the deal in good faith. Rafael ought to thank him, he supposed, but he only felt foolish that everyone seemed to have been in on the lies except him.

"I need air," he muttered and yanked open the door.

A woman was on her way in. She faltered in surprise. She was in her fifties with threads of silver in her brunette hair. Her smile was the one that he'd seen on Molly's face nearly every time he'd seen her.

"Hello, Rafael. I'm Patricia. Call me Patty." She thrust out her hand and returned his firm shake.

"Nice to meet you," he managed, but she was already dropping his hand and sweeping past him.

"Sasha," she greeted, melting with emotion as she opened her arms to envelop his wife.

Sasha embraced her, but looked over her shoulder to the empty doorway, expression haunted. "Where's—"

"Libby wanted to stay with Molly. Can you give her a day or two?" She drew back to smooth Sasha's hair. "It's not just you. She's worried about Molly and upset we didn't tell her about the baby."

Rafael was vaguely aware of Gio ghosting past him and out the door, but he was wholly focused on the way Sasha's face crumpled even as she nodded with acceptance.

His heart folded in on itself. Her agony was so tangibly his, it nearly destroyed him.

This is love, he thought. He wouldn't feel her pain so acutely if she wasn't in possession of his heart. He wanted to go to her and hold her, but she was clinging to Patricia. He understood that that was where she needed to express that particular pain, but it was more devastation than he could witness.

He stepped outside the room and closed the door, then

leaned on the wall, trying to ease the fire in his chest with slow, even breaths.

It was hitting him, though, the magnitude of responsibility Sasha had shouldered at sixteen. He had dismissed her animosity toward her mother and stepfather as a spoiled heiress who didn't like to be hemmed in. He hadn't imagined that she could understand his struggles, making adult decisions as an adolescent himself, taking over his father's business, and prying it loose from crooks.

Yet at sixteen, she'd carried a baby in secret because the adults who should have been protecting her had left her as bait for a wolf. She'd found a loving home for her baby, refusing to risk that baby suffering the abuse that she'd endured. Letting go of her baby had been so painful, she hadn't been able to speak about it for more than ten years.

He was so racked with pain on her behalf, he braced his hands on his knees, trying not to be sick.

Italian shoes and bespoke trouser cuffs came into his line of vision. He straightened to see Gio.

"Molly is awake. She wants to see her mother." He stepped past Rafael and knocked on the door, then poked his head in to deliver his message. He closed it again, looking grave. "I've arranged a hotel for Patty and Libby. I'll take them when they're ready."

"*I've* arranged a hotel," Rafael said with annoyance.

"It's one less thing on your plate and…" Gio's cheek ticked. "I'd like to look after Molly's family."

Molly's sister wasn't just *Molly's* family, though, was she?

A few hours ago, when Sasha had relayed her past to

him, all of this had been a story. Now it was real. Real people. Real heartache.

Patricia came out of the lounge and squeezed Rafael's arm.

"See if you can talk her into going home for some rest. I need to get Libby to bed, too. We'll talk more tomorrow." She had such a reassuring air about her, he wanted to catch her back and insist she come home with them.

He slipped into the lounge to see Sasha was on the couch, doubled over her folded arms. She wore a shell-shocked expression, eyes dry, but her face was ravaged by tears.

"Sash?"

She drew back when he tried to cradle her cheek and turned her face away.

"She doesn't want to see me," she said in a voice shredded by desolation. "But I can't walk away from her again. Stand in the hall and tell me when she's gone."

A chasm opened inside him. He wanted to sit down and pull her into his lap. He wanted to walk down the hall and tell that little girl to get her butt in here, but she was only a little girl. A child who had probably started her day by getting ready for school, never dreaming she would meet her birth mother today, or that her sister's life would be in danger. She had been completely ignorant of the fact she had a half brother or sister on the way.

Punch drunk from all the shocks, Rafael stepped out the door and, a moment later, Gio emerged from Molly's room with Patty. She said something in a hushed voice and held out her arm for the preteen who joined her.

Nothing could have prepared him for his first glimpse of Libby. How had he not known that she would be a version of Sasha that was like looking at his wife through a lens that saw back in time. She had Sasha's same long hair and slender build, her graceful profile, and she brushed her hair off her shoulder in exactly the same way. Her eyes were so blue he felt the splash of them when she glanced his direction.

And that expression. When she noticed he was staring at her, her brows gathered into a scowl that asked, *Who the hell are you?*

He was a man experiencing love in its most pure and innocent form. What an impudent brat! He wanted to laugh and cry and say, *Sasha, she's beautiful. She's you. Come see.*

He waited until he heard the elevator doors open and close, then he went in to gather his wife, deciding it was best to say nothing at all.

CHAPTER ELEVEN

SASHA WOKE WITH a vague memory of Rafael holding her until she fell asleep, but the apartment was empty. He'd left her a text that he was at the office and would stop by the hospital midday.

There was also a text from Molly.

Peanut is doing somersaults. Dr. says no change. Mom says I have to stagger my visitors so I can rest. I feel like I'm grounded. I didn't even stay out past curfew!

Sasha texted back.

I'll bring you a cake with a nail file.

She took her time getting ready, since it sounded as though Patty and Libby were already there. Patty had wanted to speak with the doctor first thing, so that didn't surprise her, but the pair hadn't slept much, so they had already gone back to their hotel by the time Sasha got there.

"Libby is mad at me, too," Molly said, trying to mollify Sasha. "For letting her believe my engagement was real." Her gaze darted toward the open door where Gio had disappeared.

"Why is he still here?" Sasha mouthed.

"I don't know," Molly mouthed back.

"Do you want me to—"

"No," Molly said hurriedly. "He can stay if he wants to."

When Molly grew sleepy, Sasha left, promising to come back later. She filled an hour picking up some random things for her—magazines and moisturizer, a deck of cards and a board game that was suitable for a tween. Did she want to go broke buying bribery gifts for Libby? Heck, yes.

Instead, she went home and checked in with her counselor, who said, "Time may not heal all wounds, but all wounds need time to heal."

Ugh. It was glib, but she was right.

She had just missed Patty and Libby when she went back to see Molly, but at least she was able to eat dinner with her, since Rafael had already said he would be working late.

"Do you think you two will get through this?" Molly pried gently.

"I don't know, Moll. What I did was pretty unforgivable, but…" She swallowed. "I didn't mind being married to someone who didn't love me when I didn't think I deserved to be loved. Now…"

"Sash." Molly squeezed her hand.

"Don't worry about us, okay? You're not allowed." Patty was being pretty strict about keeping Molly's cortisol levels down. "For now, the only thing I'm thinking about is you and the baby."

"And Libby?" Molly guessed.

"Yeah," Sasha admitted with a pang in her throat.

"She'll come around. And she'll be nosy as hell when she does," Molly warned with amusement.

Sasha looked forward to it.

Time slowed to a crawl, leaving her too much time to fret about her marriage, especially as Rafael didn't come home until well after midnight.

"Is everything all right at work?" she murmured when he slid into bed beside her.

"Just putting the house in order."

"The house?" She picked up her head.

"Proverbial." He hesitated, then, "No matter what happens in the next week or two, you and I will need some time."

"Oh." She dropped her head back onto the pillow. Her heart stalled, then restarted.

"That's not—I just called the hospital. They said Molly and the baby are fine. Don't worry. Go back to sleep."

She couldn't help worrying. She wanted to ask him to hold her, but they were in too precarious a place. Instead, she waited until his breathing had evened out, then let her hand creep across to rest on his arm before she was able to drift off again.

He was gone again when she woke, leaving her to turn over his words as she waited until she could go to the hospital again.

On the third day of Molly's bed rest, she was in the lounge, waiting for Patty and Libby to leave, when Libby walked in.

Sasha almost dropped her coffee.

Libby faltered, eyes widening in recognition before her gaze darted around the otherwise empty room.

"My mom said there's hot chocolate here."

"There is." Sasha stepped aside and pointed. "It's that button. How's Molly?"

"They're taking her for her scan. Mom's allowed to go with her because she's…" She shrugged.

"Pushy?" Sasha joked.

"Heh. Sometimes." Libby set the cup, then pushed the button. "She sent me here probably knowing you were here, so yeah. I guess."

"You didn't want to see me?" Sasha tried not to let that destroy her.

"I don't know." Libby picked up the full cup, tried to sip and flinched because it was too hot.

"Milk? To cool it?" Sasha suggested, pointing to the refrigerator.

Libby shook her head and set it aside, then looked to the door.

Oh, God. I have to be the adult, don't I?

It wasn't easy when she felt as though she had regressed back to the teenager she'd been the last time she saw her daughter.

"I know Pat— I mean, your mom…" Ouch. "I know your mom has explained as much as she knows about why I let her adopt you, but you can ask me anything you want. I won't be upset."

"Why didn't you come see me?" She folded her arms defensively. "Mom said that you could have."

Oof. Start with an easy one, why didn't she?

"I was afraid to," she answered simply. "I was sad and thought it would hurt too much, and that I might put you and your mom at risk, legally, from my stepfather. Mostly, I didn't feel good about myself and really believed you were better off not knowing me."

Libby wrinkled her nose. "Does that mean you'll stay away after this?"

"I don't want to. Molly and I will always be friends."
She couldn't imagine her life without her now. "I'll talk
to your mom regularly, too. I'd like to see more of you if
you're okay with that."

"Could I see the baby sometimes?"

"Yes! Absolutely! I would love that so much." She was
gushing and tried to rein it in. "I know you're angry with
me, but—"

"I'm not *angry* with you. I mean, I am," Libby clarified
with a scowl. "I'm disappointed that you didn't want to see
me before now. I'm mad at *Mom* for hiding that I'm *rich*.
Molly didn't tell me she was pregnant and even Gio lied
to me about their engagement. He said I could be a brides-
maid and everything. Rafael seems like the only person I
can trust around here, but maybe he was lying to me, too."

"About what? Did you talk to him?" she asked with astonishment.

"We played cards yesterday while we were waiting for
Moll to wake up. I asked him if you guys are getting a divorce. He said he didn't want that, but that he didn't want
to lie to me in case it didn't work out. He said everyone had
been lying to him, too, so he understands where I'm coming from. I said it would be really unfair to the baby and
also to Molly if you guys got divorced, considering everything Molly is going through."

"Yeah. I know." Sasha rubbed the ache in her sternum
and bit back asking her to repeat herself. *He said he didn't
want a divorce? Are you sure?*

"I kind of get why Molly wanted to be your surrogate,"
Libby said in a tone that was reluctantly forgiving. "And
I don't really blame you for leaving me with a grown-up
you trusted, instead of raising me yourself. I'm going to

start high school next year, and I wouldn't want to stop my life to raise a baby. I babysit sometimes and you have to pay attention the *whole time*. I'd rather travel and go to concerts and become a doctor, which takes a lot of effort and dedication."

"It does. Wow. Are you interested in medicine because of what your mom does?"

"Uh-huh. I read her textbooks sometimes. She said Moll will probably have to deliver by surgery, which sounds gross when you read about it, but it saves both the mom and the baby, which is pretty amazing."

It was terrifying, actually, but Sasha couldn't help a rush of pride at Libby's ambition. She probably didn't need to hear this, but she said it anyway.

"I bet you'll make a great doctor."

"I wish I was one already." Libby suddenly looked her age. Young. Vulnerable. Scared, even. "I really hope they'll both be okay."

"Oh, baby." Sasha abandoned her own mug and crossed to hug Libby. "Me, too."

As Libby's arms came around her, Sasha's heart swelled so big it pressed tears into her eyes, but in her periphery, she caught a movement at the door.

Rafael was there, watching them.

This had been the hardest week of Rafael's life and he'd lived some very hard weeks. This wasn't about keeping himself alive, though. At least when the odds were stacked against him in the past, he'd been able to do something. He'd been able to fight, one way or another.

There was nothing he could do to help Molly, though.

Nothing he could do to ensure his baby lived. Nothing he could say that would lift the burden of worry off Sasha.

It was horrible. It was torture for a man like him. All he could do was throw himself into work, buying time he hoped they would spend with their baby.

Please let their baby arrive safely. He didn't know how he would survive any other outcome. Sasha would be completely devastated. Everyone would. And he couldn't help feeling guilty that he had brought this about.

I thought I had to have a baby to keep you. That's how little trust I had in our marriage.

He understood that completely now, because he had the feeling their marriage wouldn't survive if their baby didn't. Which devastated him.

He came into the apartment weary from another day of hiring and delegating, analyzing projections and approving action plans. It felt wrong to relinquish this much control, but he had figured out that if he wanted his marriage to survive, he was going to have to fight for it which meant allowing his business to run itself.

"You're up," he said with surprise when he found Sasha sitting in the dimly lit living room, listening to the television.

She clicked it off and removed her sleep mask. "I couldn't sleep. I had dinner with Patty and Libby. Patty thinks they'll make the decision to deliver the baby in the next day or two."

"Oh." He poured a drink and sat down on the other end of the couch.

"She says she trusts the team and that she'll join us in the meeting when they talk about the risks, if you want."

He swore and leaned forward to set his drink on the table.

"She shouldn't have to do that," he said. "She shouldn't be here worrying about her daughter like this. What have I done, Sasha?" He stayed forward, with his elbows on his knees and pushed his hands into his hair. "What the hell have I done?"

"Rafael." She shifted so she was kneeling beside him. She stroked his back. "Blaming myself is *my* thing."

"Don't joke. Not right now."

"I'm not. Not really." Her arms looped around his shoulders as she leaned onto him. The crown of her head rested against the side of his neck. "This was a collective effort. Molly knew the risks. Patty made sure she did. We all went to those counseling sessions and none of us hit the brakes because none of us thought this would happen."

"What if she can't have children of her own after this? What if—"

"I know. I think all of those same things, but at some point, we have to forgive ourselves for not owning a crystal ball. For making mistakes and being human and wanting things that maybe we aren't meant to have."

"I *want* our baby."

"I know. Me, too."

He sat back and gathered her into his lap. She snuggled into him, leaving one arm around his neck, the other tucked against his rib cage. They sat like that a long time, holding each other.

"I wanted us to have a baby because I didn't feel secure in our relationship, either," he admitted with reluctance and shame. "I hate not feeling confident, especially when it comes to you. From the moment I saw you, you consumed me."

She started to pick up her head, taking a breath to speak,

but he slid his hand to cup her neck, silently asking her to stay still and let him finish.

"I knew immediately that you could destroy me, so I fought against allowing it." He used his thumb to stroke the soft hollow beneath her ear. "Please remember that you didn't tell me you loved me until I was so jealous of Molly, I could only see green."

"I should have told you who she was," she mumbled against his shirt.

"Yes. You should have. We both should have done a lot of things. We are in a hell of our own making, but you're right. At some point we have to forgive ourselves and each other. We can only move forward from here. I don't want to lose you, Sasha. Not because it would destroy me if you left, but because you give me a reason to live."

She tilted her head back and cupped his jaw, mouth quivering. "I love you. I will always love you, but—"

He slid his thumb to still her lips. "Wait. Let me feel that." He closed his eyes and let her words wash through him. *Love. Always.*

A helpless sob left her and she buried her face in his shoulder again.

"Love did seem like a liability." He wove his fingers into her hair so he cupped the back of her skull. "It makes you so vulnerable, it's excruciating. But these last days… As helpless as I feel, I am so freaking motivated to kill or die for you and our baby. I didn't understand that love is also power, when you let yourself feel it. When I hear you say it to me, it fills me with strength. With something so right, I'm invincible. Can you please, please feel that, too, Sash? Because I love you. I always will."

* * *

Sasha didn't want to weep. She had done enough of that lately, but these were tears of release. Of acceptance. She didn't ask him if he meant what he said. She had to believe that he did. Had to. It was the only way to embark on this new beginning of trust between them. More importantly, she had to believe she deserved his love. It was, after all, a rare and special gift from someone who was very cautious about offering his heart.

"Sash? My love? I know I took too long to say it—"

"Shh," she told him. "Let me feel it."

A choked noise left him, then his arms closed more firmly around her, keeping her safe. Impressing into her the power that he'd spoken of, the way it made her feel valued and centered and right.

When she lifted her head minutes later, she didn't speak or let him say anything. She pressed her salt-stained lips to his and they both moaned with the agony of reunion. It was a chaste, soft kiss of forgiveness that slowly grew into something more questing and generous. It was a kiss that she sank into so deeply, she didn't realize he had tipped her onto the sofa until the weight of his hips were crushing her own.

Still they kissed, letting their love pour into the other. Letting it heal them both. It was a kiss she would remember all the rest of her days. The sweetest most loving of kisses she had ever known.

But the power of their love had other facets. Hot, sharp glints that began to spark and glitter and *need*. As she grew hotter and the insistence of his erection pressed on her thigh, he picked up his head, a question in his ridiculously beautiful eyes.

Her answer was to begin unbuttoning his shirt.

A satisfied growl rumbled in his throat and his chest expanded when her hands crept inside to explore his skin. She kissed the underside of his chin and scraped her teeth against the stubble there.

"Do you want me to shave?" He rasped his palm against it.

"I want you exactly as you are."

"You are deeply, deeply precious to me, Sasha. I'm sorry that I never made that clear."

"Show me now," she whispered.

He did. He undressed her slowly and set worshipful kisses against the skin he bared. He told her how much he adored the tender spots under her breast and inside her elbow and at the crease of her thigh. He said, "I missed you."

"I missed you, too." She wasn't as patient as he was. She pushed at his clothing, arching and moaning at the luxury of his hot, hair-roughened body atop her own. "I want you inside me. I need to feel you."

She wasn't quite ready. It took a moment of shifting and caressing. Of kissing and him saying, "There's no hurry. I'll always be yours."

Then he was deep inside her, pulsing like a heartbeat. He shook and she trembled.

"I pride myself on my control, my love, but I have been wanting you very badly for a very long time."

"It's okay." She petted his back and shoulder. "You don't have to wait for me."

"The hell I don't," he grumbled. "I'd wait the rest of my life if I had to."

DANI COLLINS   197

That made her smile because in some ways he really would never change, and she loved that most about him.

Of course, he waited. He barely moved while he lovingly fondled and caressed her all over, tracing paths across her skin that left a wake of shooting stars. He kissed her until she was drowning in sensuality, intoxicated by the taste of his mouth and the thrust of his tongue.

Then she realized their bodies had begun the dance of lovemaking. This slow slide and build was them, moving in perfect accord, each drawing the other along the path of ever deepening arousal. He traced his fingers down her breast and she shivered. She opened her mouth against his bicep, delicately sucking, and his breath grew jagged.

In this moment, nothing existed but the two of them. They were utterly attuned to each other, making those small noises of acute pleasure, the ones that bordered on suffering as they fought to stay here, in this glorious place, where they were one. United. Unbreakable.

Then they did break and even then, they were indelibly together.

"I need to tell you something," Rafael said as they were getting ready for their meeting with Molly's team of specialists.

"Oh?" Sasha tensed, distracted. Patty had been right. They wanted to deliver the baby by surgery tomorrow morning and needed to discuss the various procedures, precautions, and risks today.

"I know Humbolt is supposed to hand the reins to you once you have a baby, but he's likely to contest it, so I've put my lawyers onto drawing up paperwork that forces him to move out of your properties. Your mother will continue to receive her support payments and the use of one property, but she can only send you a letter—a physical one that you can choose to open or not—twice a year, on your birthday and Christmas. Otherwise, any contact has to come from you. Humbolt will be forced out of your life completely."

"I…" She didn't know how to react. It had been on her mind that she would have to start the process, but between her real concussion and fake amnesia and worrying about Molly, she hadn't had the bandwidth. She certainly hadn't planned to be so cold-blooded and final about it.

"There's a small settlement if Humbolt goes quietly," Rafael continued. "If he makes one move toward trying to maintain control, I'll sue him for every crime I can think of from mismanagement to child abuse. You can make whatever changes you want. I just needed somewhere to put my anger," Rafael said with a grim curl of his lip.

Sasha didn't need to think about it. The fears that had kept her silent had dissipated now that she had faced them. She had her daughter back in her life and her husband was on her side. She would do anything to protect Molly and Patty, but she had a feeling Gio was also prepared to take up arms in their honor.

"Once a year is often enough to hear from my mother. Otherwise, it sounds perfect. Thank you."

The following morning, for the first time, they all gathered in Molly's room as she was wheeled out for her surgery. Patricia cuddled Libby on the sofa. Gio hovered like some sort of avenging angel.

Sasha put on a brave face, refusing to think of all those things they'd told her yesterday, but as soon as Molly was gone, she turned into Rafael's arms.

The minutes passed like hours. When sixty had gone by, they all grew restless, eyeing the clock and the door and each other.

Then the doctor walked in.

"Congratulations. You have a son. Molly is in recovery. Things went very well, but the baby will need acute care for several weeks. We'll take you to meet him in a few minutes."

Sasha wilted, held up only by Rafael's trembling strength. Then she had to let go so she could share relieved laughter and hugs with Patty and Libby. Even Gio hugged her and shook Rafael's hand, saying a heartfelt, "I'm very happy for you both."

Then she and Rafael were brought to the pediatric nursery, where they met Atticus. Libby had added his name to their short list and Rafael agreed that it suited their little fighter.

He was under a warm light in an incubator, cradled in a blanket patterned with seahorses. His diaper engulfed his desperately small form. He hadn't had time to put on weight or grow hair. His limbs were thinner than Sasha's pinky finger and wires were secured to his foot and arm and mouth.

"Put on this gown," the nurse prodded gently. "Then we'll set him on you for some skin-to-skin contact."

When Sasha came back from changing, Rafael had his enormous hand inside the incubator. Teeny, tiny fingers were curled in an attempt to hang on to the tip of his index finger. Tears were standing in Rafael's eyes, magnifying the love in them.

"Oh, love," she murmured, ready to dissolve herself. She cupped his face and kissed his damp lips. Then she sat in a rocker and opened the hospital gown, accepting the weightless duckling that was her son against the swell of her breast.

While her own tears ran freely down her cheeks, Rafael fell to his knees beside them. As his warm hand settled on her thigh and his gaze ate up both of them, her heart settled into a state of peace she hadn't known since... Well, ever. Not until now.

This level of happiness was new. It wasn't naive. She knew they had struggles ahead, especially with such a premature baby, but it was going to be okay. Somehow, it would all be okay. She believed that.

And it was.

EPILOGUE

New York, one year later...

"OH, HELLO," RAFAEL SAID, turning in the spray of the shower when Sasha slipped in to join him. "I thought you were still in Patty's room."

"Since tonight is the launch of my own initiative, I feel it would be good manners to show up on time for it."

With Patty's help, Sasha had put together a foundation to raise funds for organizations that offered resources for teen clinics and reproductive care for adolescents. Libby had decided against attending. They had made an announcement a few months ago, acknowledging that Sasha was her birth mother, but Libby didn't want to be the center of attention tonight. Not when she could have her baby brother all to herself.

They saw Libby every month or two, and Atticus always gave her the same gooey grin he gave Molly, who visited even more often. He was still behind his peers in weight and development, but very middle-of-the-percentile when they factored in his due date. He was sitting up, starting to crawl and babbled all sorts of nonsense as he bashed at his toys.

"I got some hot gossip while I was in Patty's room, though," Sasha told him as she lathered her hands and ran them across his chest. "Libby asked Patty if she could homeschool so she could spend more time in Europe with us and Molly."

"I'd like that. It always feels like there's a piece missing when she leaves."

"I'm sure Patty feels the same," she said wryly. "Gio wants to buy her and Lib a house in Genoa. Patty's on board, but she has a few clients she wants to stay and deliver first. One is a young woman who's talking about placing her baby for adoption." She lifted her brows to gauge his interest. "Patty doesn't want to get our hopes up, but she said it might be worth our meeting her."

"I'm ready to have that conversation." He paused in running the bar of soap over her curves. "Are you?"

"Yes. Even if it doesn't work out this time, yes." The first months of Atticus's life had been stressful, but he was thriving now. Rafael worked the occasional late night, but he also took lots of half days and long weekends to hang out with her and their son. When Libby was with them, they often spent their time aboard the yacht. Molly and Gio joined them when they could.

"I want another baby so I have a shot at holding my own baby," Sasha joked. "Molly's on her way here, which means the competition for Atticus has increased exponentially."

"Here?" Rafael pointed facetiously at the tiled floor of the shower.

"No, my love. Molly is not joining us for our pregame lovemaking." She slid her arms around his waist, then slithered deliciously against the silky, slippery bubbles that were running down his front. His erection stabbed at her belly. "She can have her own shower with her own husband, if that's what she wants. Between you and me, I think they're trying to make their own little Atticus."

"I wish them all the best," he said sincerely. "But go back to the part about why you joined me." His soapy hands slid from her waist to her backside.

"Nostalgia," she claimed, growing more suggestive in the way she was rubbing against him. "I looked out at the skyline and was reminded of a party many moons ago, when a very dashing man asked me to dance, then swept me away for the night." She deliberately paused and cast her gaze to the ceiling before teasing, "And a day and another night... What comes after 'debauchery' on the scale of sexual excess?"

"For us? Marriage." Lust and amusement and challenge backed up in his eyes. "Why don't we do that again?"

"Because we have children! Responsibilities. People are expecting us to show up in a couple of hours. I'm sorry, but we'll have to stick with the abridged version." She ran her hand between his thighs, liking the way he caught his breath.

Then he pivoted to press her into the wall.

"I meant marriage, *agápi mou*."

His playful, sexy kiss wiped her brain.

When he let her up for air, she said, "What...um...?"

"Will you marry me, Sasha?"

"I'd marry you every year for the rest of our lives, just so you'd know how important you are to me," she said solemnly.

"Same." He was equally grave. "But I don't need a wedding every year, just one more. Not even a big one, but a proper one, like Gio and Molly's. One with the people we love there with us. One where we promise to love each other for the rest of our lives."

"Rafael." She blinked lashes that were damp from more than the shower spray. "That would make me really happy."

"Me, too. I wish I'd thought of it sooner." He dipped his head to kiss her again. "But you're right about our being pressed for time. I'm going to hit our highlight reel hard and fast, so pay attention."

He dropped to his knees and her laughter quickly turned to a moan of joy.

* * * * *

If you couldn't get enough of
The Secret of Their Billion-Dollar Baby
then make sure you catch up with
the first instalment of the
Bound by a Surrogate Baby duet
The Baby His Secretary Carries

And why not explore these other stories
from Dani Collins?

Cinderella's Secret Baby
Wedding Night with the Wrong Billionaire
A Convenient Ring to Claim Her
A Baby to Make Her His Bride
Awakened on Her Royal Wedding Night

Available now!